ORIGINS

HULI INTERGALACTIC

LEAH R CUTTER

KNOTTED ROAD PRESS

Origins
Huli Intergalactic
Copyright © 2020 Leah Cutter
All rights reserved
Published by Knotted Road Press
www.KnottedRoadPress.com

ISBN: 978-1-64470-120-1

Cover Art:

ID 99633539 © Grandfailure | Dreamstime.com

Cover and interior design copyright © 2020 Knotted Road Press

http://www.KnottedRoadPress.com

Come someplace new…
Are you a traveler? Do you enjoy exploring strange new worlds, new cultures, new people?

Journey into the various lands envisioned by Leah Cutter.

Sign up for my newsletter and I'll start you on your travels with a free copy of my book, *The Island Sampler*.

I will never spam you or use your email for nefarious purposes. You can also unsubscribe at any time.

http://www.LeahCutter.com/newsletter/

ALSO BY LEAH R CUTTER

The Witch's Progress

Circle of Air

Circle of Water

Circle of Fire

Circle of Earth

Seattle Trolls

The Changeling Troll

The Princess Troll

The Fairy-Bridge Troll

The Troll-Demon War

The Troll-Human War

The Troll-Troll War

The Cassie Stories

Poisoned Pearls

Tainted Waters

Spoiled Harvest

Bloodied Ice

Tanish Empire Trilogy

The Glass Magician

The Desert Heart

The Ghost Dog

The Shadow Wars Trilogy

The Raven and the Dancing Tiger

The Guardian Hound

War Among the Crocodiles

The Clockwork Fairy Kingdom

The Clockwork Fairy Kingdom

The Maker, the Teacher, and the Monster

The Dwarven Wars

The Chronicles of Franklin

Franklin Versus The Popcorn Thief

Franklin Versus The Soul Thief

Franklin Versus The Child Thief

Contemporary Fantasy

Siren's Call

The Immortals' War

PREFACE

In the end, physics failed mankind. The only way to achieve interstellar travel was through magic, using beacons and portals.
Da Kao Shen, The History of Travel, *2822*

ONE

THE BEACON

AO DAN SWORE at the morning news scroll as it meandered up his screen. What, were those idiots back on Earth *trying* to destroy all of mankind? Sure, he lived on the Mars colony and might escape the worst of the (latest) wars, but the colony was barely fifty years old. It wasn't self-sufficient, in terms of neither produce nor genetics.

There wasn't anything he could do about it either. Not even if he returned to Earth. Being a warlock, even a mighty one who regularly surfed tremendous chaotic streams of power, didn't mean he had the magic necessary for mundanes to actually be able to see the miracles he performed, or even be affected by it.

The majority of humanity didn't even know that magic existed. Oh, sure, they knew the wizardry of scientists, the tweaks of genetics that bioengineering had led to, particularly over the last one hundred years, but not true enchantment.

Or real monsters.

With a wave of his hand, Ao Dan dismissed the scrolling screen that he had projected above the breakfast bar of his tiny living space. As much as he might petition the gods (and

1

he'd met more than one being of incredible power) it appeared that they couldn't change that one indisputable fact: mundanes couldn't see magic, even when it was performed in front of them. Most magical spells didn't affect them either, regardless if done by a boring, law-abiding wizard or a chaos-surfing warlock.

It seemed that mankind was destined to go to an early grave and never taste true power.

Or never escape beyond the local solar system and reach the stars.

Ao Dan stacked his chopsticks and his breakfast bowl (with the remains of the absolutely delicious garlic chicken soup still clinging to the rim) into the cleaner. He remembered when it would have been a dishwasher he used. However, while humans had discovered there was some water locked beneath the surface of Mars, there wasn't enough of it to waste on trivial things like cleaning dishes. That was much more easily accomplished by sonics.

Ao Dan didn't understand all the science. He'd just marveled at the new inventions as they came along.

Wizards, those people who reveled in merely doing as he or she was told, had a life expectancy around ninety years.

As a warlock, breaking the rules and ignoring the consequences, he could choose to live as long as he wanted.

And he planned on sticking around forever. Or at least until he found his true soulmate, Richard, reborn into another body in a new time and space, as Sun Hou-tse, the Monkey King, had promised him.

Ao Dan had once hired a computer hacker to scan all reported births for specific factors, selecting for parameters that would indicate Richard was reborn. There had been too many variables, though. Too many false positives. No way of knowing for certain if this or that squalling ball of wailing flesh would turn into the man that Richard had been.

How long before Richard was reborn? Had he already lived and died again, never crossing Ao Dan's path? It had been over two hundred years since Ao Dan had last held his love. With his magic, he could still see Richard, recall those past days with an accuracy and veracity that technology had yet to master, even with the best holograms.

Maybe today was the day. But he wasn't about to find Richard if he didn't leave his living quarters.

Like every person on Mars, Ao Dan automatically checked the air quality of the hallway before opening the hatch leading from his tiny rooms to the shared parts of the habitat. While alarms were supposed to sound if there was a breach (loud enough to wake the dead) that didn't mean that anyone actually trusted all the systems. The mantra they all lived by was, "Trust, but verify."

The mechanical dial was all green, and the magical thread that Ao Dan sent out showed that the corridor was normal, so he opened his hatch. He could survive a breach—his magic would protect him from exposure as well as the lack of oxygen. Not that he'd ever tried doing a spacewalk or a surface walk without an EVA suit.

He had tried opening his helmet once while on the surface, when far away from any camera's watchful eye. The surge of magic required to save him had destroyed most of the electronics in his suit. Fortunately, the manufacturer had replaced it immediately, and with a much higher quality one, assuming that the total system failure had been their fault (and that Ao Dan would have sued them and won).

A few colonists walked along the corridor, minding their own business and going to their various tasks. Everyone had on variations of the same outfit—tight jumpsuits that could be worn inside an EVA suit in every color of the rainbow.

You never knew when you'd have to jump into a spare suit due to a breach. The colony had "breach drills" on a regular basis. One of the idiots in charge actually opened an airlock in a random location at least once a year to make sure that people were complying.

At least the colonists had embraced color. The habitat walls and floor were all the same manufactured beige that made Ao Dan want to scratch his eyes out on a regular basis. It warmed his heart that the other colonists had felt the same way and insisted on wearing the brightest clothes they could find.

Ao Dan himself was in a suit with a bright fuchsia top that had wide gold stripes running from under his arms to the start of his thighs. A design of green leaves and vines circled his arms from cuff to shoulder. Though the outfit was a single piece, most people preferred to at least appear to be wearing pants, so the legs of Ao Dan's outfit were a much darker red, with the same pattern of leaves and vines circling his calves.

He kept his hair buzzed short, like most people did, again, necessity driving fashion.

What no one knew was that only half of his hair would ever grow back. He'd given the other half to the Monkey King, a token that bound him to the chaotic god, a cheap enough price for the promise of being reunited with Richard.

Ao Dan nodded at a few of the people he recognized, but he wasn't forced to actually talk to anyone that morning, always a bonus. Or maybe the other colonists had grown tired of the growls and grunts that he gave to even the politest of small talk.

Most of the other colonists were short like Ao Dan, who was barely five eight, his Chinese heritage showing in the fold of his black eyes and his darker skin. Only a few had that willowy height and slight build that indicated they were natives to the planet.

Being a wizard, or even a warlock, didn't mean that Ao

Dan automatically had enough money to eat. He had saved and invested judiciously so he could get by for a decade or more without working. However, just practicing magic all day in his private room grew dull after a while.

When Ao Dan had first read about the proposed colony, he'd enrolled in computer and equipment repair classes, seeking to acquire the sorts of skills that a colony would require.

However, his magic didn't work well with computers.

When he'd been a wizard, following the strict rule of law, his power could be tolerated by the delicate electronics.

After becoming a warlock and harnessing the untamed, natural magic, he'd frequently blown out whatever machine he was working on.

It took a while for Ao Dan to find the perfect career that he could tolerate, that would require him to spend most of his time alone, and that the colonists would desperately need. It had required years of study, but he had spent the time to become an ichthyologist who could do double-duty as an aquaponics engineer, *and* who also had studied just enough botany to be dangerous.

Ao Dan ran the fish farm for the colony with an iron fist. No one was allowed into the aquaponic lab—just think what germs or diseases they might be carrying! It was far too easy for the fish to just die and the colony be out of luck.

Plus, he'd finally figured out how to transport more creatures from Earth through a magical portal if he accidentally killed one (or more) of the long troughs of fish and hadn't collected enough eggs to reseed his harvest.

It was only possible to create a portal to a location that the magician had physically been in. The Monkey King had actually helped Ao Dan do this once, transporting him to the middle of one of the Great Lakes so that he could capture the freshwater fish he needed.

The controls outside the door to the lab showed everything was normal on the inside. The hatch to the fish farm ran on a separate power grid, supposed to isolate and protect the lab in case of serious system failure through the rest of the colony.

What good was it if the humans survived by jumping into suits, but their food supply died?

Ao Dan actually didn't need the redundant human systems. He'd set up a magical fallback himself, that he regularly renewed, so that if there was that sort of catastrophic breach the lab itself would be safely transported to a pocket world, the fish and the tanks held in stasis until the emergency was over.

The lab smelled green and wet, a welcome respite from the dry air of the rest of the colony. Ao Dan missed the smells of Earth more than he'd thought he would. Dark green walls suited the lab, better than the plain gray that they'd originally come in. It had been one of the few magical effects that Ao Dan had managed to pull off that the rest of the colonists could actually see.

The control room was located up one level from the long troughs of fish, below. Again, redundant systems, not just to control breaches but disease. Fish died surprisingly easily. Even ones who'd been genetically "hardened." Before Ao Dan could enter the farm itself, he had to go through an extra sonic cleansing cycle in the airlock. It always made his skin itch in the most irritating manner. More than once he'd had to stop himself from just blasting the thing to pieces.

Two huge tanks of fish dominated the control room, plus over a dozen smaller tanks that lined the walls. One of the big tanks was for control groups that Ao Dan used for his experiments. The other was filled with colorful tropical fish. Ao Dan had justified the expense to the colony by claiming that the saltwater fish had interesting characteristics that could be used to genetically engineer the freshwater fish into stronger, healthier farmed breeds.

While Ao Dan hadn't been making up all his claims out of whole cloth, he'd mainly wanted the tank for its beauty.

Ao Dan quickly verified that all was running well in the fish farm, below. His morning screen feed always included a rolling band of text at the bottom indicating all the important stats, like oxygen levels in the water, filtering systems capacity, estimated number of fish, and so on. Alarms would have sounded in his living quarters if something had gone terribly wrong. Still, he always checked first thing.

Today, he'd harvest half of one of the tanks. While the most humane method to kill the fish was to electrify the mesh encasing the bottom of the trough, Ao Dan found it much simpler to run a magical charge through the water, then lift the fish out instead of having to drain the water to reap his kill.

Ao Dan decided he would have one more cup of tea before starting his morning work. The smell of jasmine filled the air as the empty cup in front of him slowly filled. He sat down behind his desk, grimacing at the paperwork that just never ended. However, instead of starting up that mountain, he glanced at the newsfeed from Earth.

And cursed again.

He was going to have to figure out how to get humanity to *not* blow themselves up before they had achieved something akin to faster than light travel. It was the only way humanity might survive its stupider instincts.

But how?

***

IT HAD SURPRISED Ao Dan that he wasn't able to use a

portal himself to go back to Earth whenever he wanted. Transporting the fish had actually taken quite a bit of experimenting to discover how to hold not one, but two portals open simultaneously, then link them together.

Maybe if he knew of another magician who he could work with, he might be able to transport himself. But there weren't any other magicians in his part of the Mars colony. Maybe one person in one hundred had the ability to do magic, and of those, only one in a hundred thousand received the right training. The colony itself barely supported two thousand souls.

Plus, Ao Dan couldn't just go looking for other magicians. Chances were, any who found him would immediately try to kill him. He was a warlock, after all. No longer a rule-bound, goodie-two-shoes wizard.

Most of the wizards and other beings of power down on Earth worked for the *Huli* Transport corporation. They delivered messages and packages between the gods, eventually incorporating a regular, mundane shipping arm as well. The company had been started in mainland China, working for the immortals, gods, heroes, and other supernatural beings there before expanded internationally, and now had offices in many other countries and pantheons.

As a warlock, one the company had sworn to kill, Ao Dan had had to find other work.

After spending the day at the fish farm, doing his duty as a good little cog, Ao Dan decided he could handle a little bit of human contact, and so headed to the closest drinking hole. Of course, good little scientists didn't drink or need to blow off steam. The original designers of the habitat hadn't thought to include such a facility.

It had been the first thing the colonists had created, repurposing one of their community rooms.

What, had the bureaucrats who'd approved the final

designs actually believed that the colonists would only gather together to do healthy things like dancing or singing?

It still made Ao Dan snigger.

The alcohol served in Meeting Room 2, or M2 as everyone called it, wasn't exactly rotgut. There were enough chemists and engineers to modify the spirits to make them tolerable. The botanists had also been all in, supplying "leftover" clippings of herbs and other ingredients to infuse what was being produced.

The most recent cider that Ao Dan had tried—a hibiscus-lavender-cucumber—had tasted like a lovely combination of tea and alcohol.

It still didn't compare to the smoky, oak-aged Chardonnay that he'd enjoyed back on Earth.

If the colony survived, and Earth didn't blow themselves up, maybe he could go back someday to have some again. Likely, he'd have to fake his own death on Mars first, kill a departing colonist and take his place. He'd stolen some poor schmuck's identity more than once. It was a handy way for someone his age to be "reborn" younger, as well as to stay hidden from the *Huli* Transport wizards and assassins.

He generally picked a man who was known to be straight. That way, going through a crisis of orientation would explain why he'd left all his old friends behind and started a new life. And while most magic didn't work on mundanes, the sort of illusion required by a disguise could be made to "stick", at least for long enough.

The lights in M2 were purposefully kept dim, like any self-respecting dive. Tables and chairs were scattered to the right of the door, about half filled with other colonists, while the bar itself took up much of the wall on the left. Only a few stools were located there. Currently, none of them were occupied.

The bar didn't look like a bar, not really. Instead, it was

just a repurposed counter that had quickly gotten scratched to hell by all the use. Only a few actual bottles lined the shelf behind the counter. Instead, the colonists had fixed up a series of hand-made taps connected to the hidden barrels of booze, which were kept at the perfect temperature at all times (scientists who turned their hands to alcohol were even more persnickety than most).

"Hello, Andy," Shivesh, the bartender on duty, said as Ao Dan came up. "How are you?"

Ao Dan kept his grimace hidden. While most of the colonists would use his proper name, some still insisted on using an Americanized version, particularly those from India. It came in handy when dealing with those who bore scars from the previous war with China.

Ao Dan had been born American, in the Midwest. He was used to spending his life in hiding, though: first, disguising the fact that he was gay, then his true vocation as a wizard, and after breaking all his oaths and becoming a warlock, even more so.

"I'm doing fine, Shivesh," Ao Dan replied when he realized that the idiot bartender actually expected a reply.

Maybe he didn't have such a great need for human company after all.

Still, since he was here…

"What's the cider of the day?" Ao Dan asked. He knew he was being rude not asking after Shivesh and his precious apple crop. The other colonist did provide much of the base materials for the alcohol, after all.

"I have two options," Shivesh said, nodding. Maybe he was used to colonists not wanting to spend that much time talking and instead just concentrated on their drinking.

Shivesh reached out and put a finger on a tap that had probably come from a 3-D printer and looked like a spruce tree. "This one is a pine cider. Uses the best of both the apple and the fir."

Ao Dan shuddered. Sounded horrific, like a sweetened industrial cleaner. "And the other?"

Shivesh grinned at him, then pointed to a tap that was as white as bone and looked like the delicate veins of a leaf after the rest of it had rotted away. "Ice wine cider," he announced proudly. "It took me very long to find the balance between the two sweets. To combine both tastes."

"I'll try that," Ao Dan said. "Just put it on my tab."

Officially, the colony didn't really run on money. The colonists did the necessary work, and the colony itself supplied them with food, oxygen, and a place to stay.

Unofficially, deals were always being made. A few fish might "fall" out of the long troughs on their way to the official processing plant and into the hands of the colonists who could supply Ao Dan with special goods. The most precious thing to barter for was space on the next supply shipment.

"I will do that," Shivesh said, nodding.

Ao Dan knew that the botanist actually kept close tabs on who was drinking what, and how much. It wouldn't do for someone to be unable to function anymore. They were still too interdependent for that sort of slip up.

The first sip surprised Ao Dan. Shivesh had been right. The cider started off with the higher, sweeter flavor of the ice wine, then mellowed with the more sour apple at the back.

Ao Dan raised his glass in salute to the bartender before ambling off to one of the empty tables. He'd planned originally on sitting at the bar, but now he had the feeling that he needed to be at a table, as if waiting for someone.

As usual, his instincts paid off.

"Mind if I sit here for a while?" came a melodic voice, speaking Mandarin.

Ao Dan couldn't help but smile. "Please, do," he said, pulling out the chair for the other being.

He wondered what the other people in the bar saw, if they saw anything at all.

At least he never had to explain to anyone how he would sometimes meet with Sun Hou-tse, the Monkey King.

WHEN AO DAN had first met the Monkey King, he'd introduced himself as Sunny. Ao Dan had called him by that name ever since.

Sunny wore one of the brightest jumpsuits Ao Dan had ever seen, as usual. The top was done in a Hawaiian print, with a bright blue background and red and white hibiscus flowers. The bottom was an even louder print, with bright gold and green geometric patterns.

On most people, the patterns and colors would have clashed horribly. On Sunny, they almost worked. Not that Ao Dan was going to offer the god fashion commentary, no matter how much he might be tempted.

Sunny still had bright yellow hair that he wore much longer than any colonist, curling down to his shoulders. Ao Dan was never sure why Sunny chose that hair, if it reminded him of something or if it was just his favorite wig. He had a very flat, human-looking face, like a cartoon character, though his eyes were tiny. His skin was dark, almost brown. He had very large hands for someone his size, broad and meaty.

"What brings you to the colony?" Ao Dan asked as he sipped his drink.

A glass materialized in Sunny's hand, filled with a clear amber liquor. He took his own sip before he replied. "You've seen the news, yes? About the idiots on Earth?"

"I have," Ao Dan said, grimacing. "There wouldn't happen to be something you could do?"

Sunny shook his head. "While I'm all for the end of law, the cost of this latest war is too high for even me to bear."

Ao Dan nodded. He'd heard Sunny state similar sentiments before. While war brought a certain level of chaos, what good was it if everyone died as a result?

"Plus, anything I tried, well, would probably lead to more war. Not more law," Sunny also admitted after a moment with a huge grin.

"True," Ao Dan said. That was the problem with worshipping chaos. It did tend to lead to things like wars and a breakdown of society. If Sunny tried to help those idiots on Earth, chances were, the chaos that ensued would be much worse.

"I do have a plan, though," Sunny said. "It would require a favor from you."

Ao Dan stiffened. As part of his original bargain with Sunny, he'd agreed to do "favors" for the Monkey King now and again.

Sunny had assured him at the time that the favors that he asked of Ao Dan would be things that Ao Dan would actually do himself, a desire that he'd act on, given a chance.

For the most part, Sunny hadn't lied. The little things Ao Dan had done for the god, while not necessarily legal or lawful, had been things that Ao Dan had wanted to do.

But then there had been that boy in Thailand.

Sunny had requested that Ao Dan seduce him. While Ao Dan was close to one hundred at the time, he still appeared as a young man in his thirties. The boy had been legal, though just barely eighteen.

Pradsung had been gorgeous, with that supple, smooth skin of youth. Ao Dan had happily gone to work on the boy, posing as a rich, Chinese foreigner who was hiring a "companion" for his travels.

It had been sweet at first, that slow seduction. Those first few, hesitant kisses.

It was only later that Ao Dan had started to have doubts. How the boy had cried after his first hand job. How he'd resisted going all the way, either penetrating or being penetrated.

Ao Dan would never forget the meeting he'd had with Sunny, on the balcony of the suite he'd rented, Pradsung behind him in the room, sprawled out across the bed, lightly snoring. The moon had just risen and they looked out over lush, shadowed forests. Cicadas sang in the distance, and the humid, warm air lay like a soft blanket over everything.

Sunny had insisted that Ao Dan needed to claim the boy fully as his. He'd arranged for two other boys to come in that evening. They all needed to be deflowered completely and utterly debased.

Ao Dan told himself afterward that it hadn't been rape. Not really. All the boys would have given in eventually, talked into giving their assent. Eventually.

But neither Pradsung nor Ao Dan had wanted to wait. They'd both been too caught up in the moment, not realizing the damage they'd done until the tears and recriminations had started.

It turned out that not only had both of the boys been virgins, Pradsung's soul had also been virginal. This was the first time his soul had taken material form. It had never had a previous human lifetime.

The stain Pradsung had put on his soul by taking his pleasure as he had would follow him through all his reincarnations, marking him as one of the Monkey King's until he finally cleansed himself of it by doing enough good deeds.

Sunny hadn't asked for another "favor" for decades, and never again asked for something so distasteful.

"What kind of a favor do you need from me this time?" Ao Dan said, not hiding how wary he felt.

For the first time that meeting, Sunny lost his casual grin. "It's a big one," he admitted seriously.

"As big as Thailand?" Ao Dan said pointed.

Sunny shrugged before he finally said in a very quiet voice, "Possibly bigger."

Ao Dan shivered. "Why," he stated flatly.

"Because it's the only way I can think of to give you idiots the stars." The Monkey King sounded angry. "While I might enjoy watching you blow yourselves back to the stone age, there's no guarantee that you'd survive this time. And what good is the circus without the clowns?" He gave a crooked grin. "I'd like to blow this pop stand. And take most of humanity with me."

Ao Dan knew that he'd never get the full story on why the Monkey King wanted to leave the local solar system. Was there yet another war with the gods that the Monkey King was losing? Or did he have some bet going?

It didn't matter, because Ao Dan knew that his own strongest desire was to achieve the stars as well.

"What is the cost?" Ao Dan had to ask.

Sunny made a balancing motion with his two hands, reenacting a scale. "One man's life, versus the stars."

Ao Dan knew that whatever Sunny was asking for, it wouldn't be as easy as killing a man. Ao Dan had done that more than once, and with no regrets.

But something worse than corrupting a youth?

Just how low was Ao Dan willing to go in order to achieve his dearest held ambition? To live forever out among the stars? As well as to survive long enough until he met his Richard again?

The fact that this one man's life in the balance would also save the rest of humanity was just a bonus as far as he was concerned.

"I'll do it," Ao Dan said slowly. "But. You can't ask me for another favor for centuries."

"Done," Sunny said. He looked grateful, an odd look that Ao Dan had never before seen on the face of the god.

"Now, you'll have to work quickly," Sunny said, "before those idiots start their war."

"And do what?" Ao Dan asked.

"Show him the portals," Sunny directed. His features were starting to shift, growing watery. "He's close enough to be able to see your magic."

"Who?" Ao Dan said. Damn it! Why did Sunny insist on being so obscure most of the time?

Sunny gave him a thumb's up signal just before his features completely transitioned away.

A different man now sat at Ao Dan's table, a colonist Ao Dan hadn't met before. He was a white man, with dark curly hair and dark eyes. He had the look of a runner, lean and hungry. Or maybe a whippet, with that sharp chin and nose. His jumpsuit was fairly conservative, until he moved, and Ao Dan realized it wasn't a solid black, but had silver woven into it, and a pattern of stars.

"Thanks for inviting me to sit with you," the man said, sticking his hand out. "I'm Henry."

"Ao Dan," he said automatically. "I'm in charge of the fish farm," he added.

Henry grinned. "Good," he said. "I've spent too much time working with theoretical scientists. Came out here to rub elbows with those who are actually doing the work."

"And your work is?" Ao Dan asked, bemused. Henry seemed like a typical geek.

"Engineering astrophysics," Henry said. "Looking for the

physics to make our spaceship engines faster. Experimental transitions of material. Maybe even taming a wormhole. Need to figure out how to prove that Einstein wasn't right."

"Fascinating," Ao Dan said, already regretting his bargain. Henry was one of those geeky scientists who was going to talk about his work all the damned time.

Ao Dan suddenly wondered if the pain of this bargain wasn't going to involve taking Henry's life, but instead, having to put up with the man and not kill him beforehand.

WEN HO, Ao Dan's original mentor back on Earth, had predicted that the chaotic magic was going to change Ao Dan in ways that he didn't know or appreciate. Bad ways.

At first, Ao Dan noticed that he'd grown more cruel, less patient and understanding. Then again, he'd never had that much sympathy for the common man.

However, Wen Ho had been wrong, or rather, he hadn't realized that Ao Dan hadn't just taken up with the chaotic magic for the sake of the massive amount of power afforded to him.

No, Ao Dan had a specific goal: to live long enough to meet Richard reborn. In addition, Wen Ho hadn't realized that Ao Dan had a surefire method to hold himself in check, which was to travel back in time to watch Richard, to be with him, to remind himself why he was doing this.

The first time Ao Dan had gone into the past and found his present self sneering at Richard when he said something loving, Ao Dan had spent a week isolated at a monastic retreat on a mountaintop. The cells hadn't been heated, and the food had been the same beans and rice, day after day.

But the air had been clear, and the monks had let Ao

Dan sit for hours on a cold stone bench, gazing out over the vista and asking himself what he really wanted.

The nature of the chaotic magic was going to change him. He couldn't help that. So would living for so long.

But what good was it to live long enough to meet Richard again, only to have become someone who could no longer love? Or more importantly, who Richard would no longer love in return?

Ao Dan could see himself falling into the easy path of cruelty and hatred, instead of doing the hard work of understanding.

He vowed never to become that man.

Sure, he would have some black stains on his soul. That was just part of being human. He would make the wrong decision, more than once.

He also swore to learn from his mistakes, and Sunny learned not to push once Ao Dan drew a line in the sand. Sunny actually seemed to respect that Ao Dan had limits, unlike some of the other followers of Sun Hou-tse who Ao Dan had met.

So in the two-hundred-plus years since Richard's death, Ao Dan had never grown as cruel as he could have, never as heartless or mean as Wen Ho probably expected. Ao Dan knew he'd changed. Life was going to do that to him. He would never be the exact same Ao Dan who had first fallen in love with Richard. Richard who had been out of the closet since he'd been a boy, with his parents supporting him. Richard who had been brave enough to love Ao Dan, and to believe in him, even though he couldn't ever see the magic Ao Dan performed.

Richard who'd had his life stolen from him by a cheating ex who'd given him AIDS.

Richard had made Ao Dan promise to not become a

hermit, to go out and live his life fully. Maybe even fall in love again.

To be happy.

Ao Dan had done the best he could.

For the sake of Sunny's plans, as well as saving the rest of humanity, Ao Dan was willing to put his own immediate happiness to the side, at least for the time being. Instead, he focused on securing Henry's trust, first as a colonist then as a lover.

Turned out, Henry was a giggler. He was gentle and kind during sex, and frequently laughed during and after orgasm. He was also extremely ticklish, a trait Ao Dan exploited ruthlessly to get Henry to agree to things.

Like today.

"I'm still not sure what you want me to see," Henry said, looking around the clean room that Ao Dan had bartered to "borrow" for an hour.

The clean room had special filters on the air systems so no dust would enter the room. They wore full suits so they wouldn't contaminate the space with errant hairs, flecks of skin, or even their breath. The cameras had been conveniently rerouted so that they'd show an empty space, as had the rest of the sensors.

They were as alone as they could be outside of their habitat. The plain, white walls held fewer electronics and gadgets as well, so it was one of the safer places where Ao Dan could practice his magic.

Ao Dan had tried bringing Henry to his magical practice room, a space that he'd carved out of a pocket world and was accessed through the back of his one closet. However, Henry had fallen asleep immediately on stepping into the room, as Richard always had.

"Here," Ao Dan said, handing Henry a small, non-reactive metal cube. He was familiar with it from his own experiments, and held it in one hand while watching Ao Dan carefully.

Ao Dan sprinkled ash in a circle on one of the counters. He didn't have to look at Henry to know the stink eye he'd be getting, bringing in such a material here. There wasn't anything for it, however.

Concentrating, reciting the spell from memory, Ao Dan created a very small portal, maybe one foot tall and half that wide. It took on the familiar shape of a regular, law-abiding portal, a blue oval with small streaks of lightning randomly flashing around the edges, with the middle a swirling black abyss. (He wasn't about to try this as a chaotic portal that glowed with bright fire. Those were a lot more difficult to control.)

Ao Dan looked over his shoulder at Henry.

Who stared fascinated at the portal.

Despite Sunny's assurances, Ao Dan hadn't believed that Henry would be able to see anything, as he hadn't appeared to have noticed any of the other magic Ao Dan had performed in front of him.

Seemed Sunny was right. Henry could see, or at least sense, portals.

"What do you see?" Ao Dan asked quietly.

Henry appeared to shake himself back to the present. "A black hole. A miniature black hole. How did you do that? What sort of projection are you using?" He stomped forward and waved his hands angrily around the portal, as if seeking to disrupt the light source. "Is it coming from underneath the table?" he asked, squatting down and looking, running his hands over the floor.

"No," Ao Dan said quietly. "It's a portal. It's magic."

The eyeroll Henry gave him was easily seen even with the helmet he wore.

"Come back here," Ao Dan said, exasperated when

Henry continued to see if he could find a source for what he was certain was just a hologram.

"Fine," Henry said walking back to stand beside Ao Dan. He still held the cube in his hand. "I suppose you want me to toss this through the black hole."

"Not yet," Ao Dan said. He went through the same incantation, sprinkling more ash, as he set up a second portal at the other end of the table, about six feet away from the first.

On the one hand, Ao Dan was pleased that Henry was able to see the second portal as well, given the way he stared at it.

On the other hand, it disturbed Ao Dan how Henry appeared to be mesmerized by what he called a black hole.

Ao Dan then used a third, different incantation to link the two portals together. It was fairly easy, as they were in the same room and not, say, on different planets.

Or even different galaxies.

"Now, toss the cube into the one on the left," Ao Dan said. "It will come back out through the one on the right."

Henry grimaced, but did as he was told.

Travel between the two portals wasn't simultaneous. It did, however, only take a faction of a second.

Henry nodded to himself, before trying it again, only reversing the order, pushing the cube into the portal on the right and watching it tumble out of the portal on the left.

"What would happen if I stuck my hand in there?" Henry asked.

Ao Dan had tried that himself, once. It had been an incredibly unpleasant feeling, the edge of the portal surrounding his arm like a stabbing curtain of ice.

"Same thing as what happens with the cube," Ao Dan assured him. "It doesn't feel good," he warned. However, he knew that Henry had to try it for himself.

Slowly, Henry's gloved fingers entered the one portal. He grimaced and shivered, announcing, "Gods, that's cold."

It didn't stop him, though, from reaching his full arm in. His hand popped out of the far portal, his fingers wiggling and waving at him the entire time.

Henry pulled his arm out and abruptly turned on Ao Dan. "How did you do that?" he demanded. "What sort of drug did you give me? It was from one of those tropical fish, wasn't it?"

Ao Dan laughed and shook his head. "No. It's magic," he insisted.

"Can't be," Henry said, turning determinedly back toward the portals, still glowing on the table. "Has to just be some physics we don't understand yet."

"You're welcome to try," Ao Dan said softly. "But it's magic."

"Why are we here in the clean room?" Henry asked, suddenly suspicious. "Can you do this anywhere else?"

"Anywhere you choose," Ao Dan said. "I did it here because the magic is less likely to interact with the electronics here. I won't blow things up accidentally."

"I see," Henry said, narrowing his eyes at Ao Dan for a moment before turning back to the portal.

Ao Dan sighed. He was going to have to get used to feeling like a bug under a microscope for a while.

Eventually, though, he knew that Henry would believe him. Would understand that it was magic, and nothing else. That those black holes were portals. Einstein was still right.

Ao Dan also knew that he'd lose Henry once he made that shift, that Henry would stare too long into the abyss.

Suddenly, the "favor" that Sunny was asking for made more sense.

One man's sanity for the stars.

It was still a bargain, or so Ao Dan told himself.

"JUST ONE MORE LOOK," Ao Dan said quietly, bringing Henry's attention back to the "lab" they sat in.

It hadn't taken long for Henry to come around to believing Ao Dan's magic. However, he had seemed personally affronted that just the portals themselves weren't the answer.

A magician could only create a portal to someplace that they'd personally visited. Just pictures of a place wouldn't do.

Henry was determined to create beacons, like lighthouses, that a magician could find magically and use for the base of a portal. He envisioned drone ships seeding the universe with a network of beacons. They would travel slowly, but continuously, going far beyond the borders of where man had traveled to. They would be automated ships, dropping beacons as they sailed across the universe, building the yellow brick road that future travelers could go along later.

Ao Dan had created a vacuum tank for Henry. It was just an old fish tank, repurposed. However, Ao Dan had filled it with the absolute cold and weightlessness of space so that Henry had a place to test his theories.

Every night. Ao Dan would create a portal in the fish tank for Henry to study. He only needed the one for much of his study.

When they'd petitioned to move in together, they'd been able to upgrade from a single space to a double. Both Ao Dan and Henry had sweetened the deal, bargaining what they could, and so had snagged a two bedroom for just the pair of them. The spare bedroom had been dedicated to the building of prototypes. The portal "lab" took up part of the expanded kitchen area that Ao Dan had closed off with screens, generating his portals on the countertop, well away from the oven and other electronics so they didn't fry.

At first, Henry would happily stare into the abyss, then turn and scribble madly on pads that would automatically transfer the handwriting to the computer. He was discovering a new science, Ao Dan knew, one that would further all communications through the vacuum of space.

Lately, Henry had slowed down. He'd stare into space instead of at the portal, and his scribbling had taken on a nonsense quality. Henry had always loved math puzzles as well as number games. Ao Dan had discovered that instead of solving the puzzles now, Henry merely wrote random numbers into the squares. In the last week, he'd started filling all the squares with the number nine.

Ao Dan slowly pushed Henry's head so that his eyes fell back upon the black abyss of the portal.

In many ways, it was worse than the boy in Thailand, because what Ao Dan did would never bring Henry pleasure —it would just drive him insane. And Ao Dan couldn't blame anyone but himself for forcing the man to go far beyond his human capacity.

Henry gasped as he stared, then started frantically nodding as if he was listening to a stream of words from the gods themselves pouring out of the inky blackness.

Maybe he was. Maybe that was the only way for the beings of power to speak with a mere mortal.

Then again, Ao Dan suspected that he, too, would go crazy staring too long into the abyss. Nietzsche had warned them.

Henry turned away from the portal abruptly and started to write equations that made no sense to Ao Dan, but that had Henry humming along. He'd invented symbols to represent the new math and physics he was discovering.

Eventually, though, Henry would start to slow, the

numbers falling away, his eyes growing hazy and losing their focus. He'd end up just sitting, staring at nothing, until Ao Dan forced him to look one more time.

It was close enough to lights out anyway. Ao Dan collapsed the portal, then gently took the pen and board from Henry's hands, setting them on the counter. That seemed to wake the taller man.

"What? No. I can work some more," Henry insisted. He shook his black curls which Ao Dan had kept carefully trimmed. Henry still had that lean and hungry look, all his features grown sharper over the last few weeks.

"It's time for bed," Ao Dan said gently, taking Henry's hand and standing.

After a moment of initial resistance, Henry grimaced and rose up. "I'm so close," he whispered as he stood, swaying.

Ao Dan paused for a moment. Henry had said before that he was close, then something would block him and he'd start down a new path.

This time, Henry still appeared to be listening to those faraway voices that he was trying to reach with his beacons.

"Tomorrow, the other lab," Henry announced. He shook his head, coming all the way back to the present and smiling sadly at Ao Dan. "And maybe some fooling around later?"

"Of course, my love," Ao Dan assured him, though orgasms no longer made Henry laugh, but instead, made him weep uncontrollably, as if completely overwhelmed.

Hand in hand, they made their way to the small bed they'd shared for six months now. In the morning, Henry would hopefully be able to pull himself together well enough to go do the job he'd hired onto at the colony. Those days still happened regularly enough. Ao Dan knew that Henry would eventually no longer be able to work, and the colony couldn't support him. Wouldn't support him, and would insist that he be shipped back to Earth.

It would be a death sentence, one that Ao Dan wasn't sure he would regret. Death might be kinder for Henry at that point.

IN THE SPARE bedroom of their living quarters that they'd dedicated to a physical lab, Henry built prototypes of the beacon he envisioned. His most recent iteration was shaped like a stylized onion, with a broad base and a tube at the top, two feet at the bottom and almost two feet tall.

It sat on the middle of the workbench they'd built. Wires, connectors, circuitry, and boards had all been neatly put away in their separate mesh cubes. All the tools awaited Henry's hand, placed carefully on the mesh stretched on the wall above the workbench. The room still smelled of solder and melted plastic.

In one corner sat a small 3-D printer, two feet square. The newer models were so much faster than the older ones Ao Dan remembered, able to produce a custom component three inches square in under an hour. If they needed something bigger than that, they'd have to go use the general one available to all colonists, as well as explain why.

That night, Henry picked up the prototype sitting in the middle of his workbench and relegated it to the corner, with the other failed and abandoned models. He paused for a moment, looking over what he had there, then picked up a different version.

It was a tall metal pole, four feet long and half a foot in diameter. It rested on a solid square base that was two feet on a side. Ao Dan wasn't certain why the shape of the beacon was so important, beyond esthetics, but Henry had insisted that it was, that he couldn't just build a black box. The beacons needed to have a base with a tube-like top.

Once Ao Dan had made certain that Henry was contentedly tinkering away with his latest wiring and corrections, he left him on his own and went back to the main room of their living space, taking a deep breath as he sat again, relishing the quiet of the evening.

Just for a night, he wasn't having to waste his own power, generating portals, and exhausting himself. He wasn't having to actively corrupt Henry, driving him further into madness. Instead, Ao Dan had the opportunity to relax, catch up on his reading, going through some of the most recent articles that other ichthyologists had published, finding the latest recommendations for new hybrid plants for his fish.

Ao Dan lost himself in his study, filling up his empty cup with jasmine tea as the evening went on. He remembered evenings like this with Richard, each working companionably on their own projects before sweetly coming together later at night.

He knew better than to allow himself to wish that he had more evenings like this.

A deep bell-like tone brought Ao Dan out of his study. He blinked and looked around. Had that been some sort of alarm that had just rung? Had there been a breach?

Before he could call up his screen, the tone sounded again. Only this time, Ao Dan realized that he hadn't actually heard it through his ears. He'd felt it, instead, along his jawbone.

Rising quickly, he raced into the lab.

Henry stood there with a great grin on his face. He'd changed the shape of the prototype he'd been working on. Instead of a tube rising out of a solid box, the bottom base was now a disk, three feet across and only a few inches deep around the edges, rising about a foot to a peak in the center.

"You could hear that, couldn't you?" Henry asked triumphantly.

"I could," Ao Dan said, nodding.

"I didn't hear anything," Henry said. "Only you could. Probably no one else in the colony could either, unless they practiced magic."

Ao Dan had no idea how Henry knew that. Or how he'd be able to prove it.

"Now, pay attention," Henry said, picking up a small round remote control with a single button in the center of it.

The tone sounded again, ringing in Ao Dan's head. It wasn't any louder, even though he was now in the same room as the machine.

However, Ao Dan did feel it stronger along his left jawline than on his right, starting up near his ear. A thick gold ring pierced that ear. It had been a gift from Richard, that Ao Dan had enchanted to be a sort of magical battery, where he could store extra power.

Ao Dan had other magical batteries, but only one that he carried with him all of the time.

"And again," Henry said, pressing the button once more.

This time, Ao Dan closed his eyes and called up a scrying spell. It wasn't a real test, as he knew the machine was right there. Still, he tried to find it by sound alone, following that ringing along his jaw and his earring.

The first incantation Ao Dan tried didn't work. But the second did. He could pinpoint the exact location of the ringing sound with a spell, modifying the original chant to focus more on sound than on sight.

"This might work," Ao Dan said cautiously as he opened his eyes. He had no idea how Henry had managed to create something completely mundane that still interacted with magic. What did that say about the nature of magic? Someday, could it be replicated by those who were mundane?

"What's next?" Ao Dan asked, putting aside his philosophical conundrum for later.

The way Henry's eyes lit up made Ao Dan wary. Which was saying something for a warlock who worshipped chaos.

"Field test."

HENRY INSISTED on building three of the prototypes, then tinkering with them as he made improvements to the wiring. Finally, he'd been forced to go with what he had, as his deadline had finally arrived. He'd petitioned to go observe at the telescope on the space station located in orbit.

The prototypes had stood in the center of the lab, all in a row, for a while. The final version looked like bright steel stanchions with a round base as well as a ball on top of the metal pole. Ao Dan could just imagine a red velvet rope connecting them together, a line leading through the darkness of space.

Henry's field test involved placing each one at a different observatory. As Ao Dan had always focused on fish and life on the ground, he'd never been to any of the observatories. It was actually a good test. They'd done what they could testing around the colony itself, Henry tinkering as he improved the distance the signal carried.

Ao Dan waited in their shared living space for Henry's message that the beacons had been activated. Henry was planning on placing a beacon in three different observatories, each one further away from the habitat. Part of the test was to judge distance: how far away could one of the beacons be and Ao Dan still be able to locate it?

The last few days had been almost normal. Henry still had bad periods where he got lost and stared into space, but he hadn't requested Ao Dan form a portal for him to study.

Maybe he could recover from this.

Henry's message was a single word, "Green." That meant

that he'd not only placed all of the beacons, but that they were all doing their job, pinging silently away. Neither of them was worried about existing sensors on Mars being able to pick up the sound on any of their monitored frequencies: as far as Henry could tell, the machines operated silently. The noise they made crossed a weird barrier between the human and magical range.

They were a failure in terms of normal science and physics, as currently understood by man.

For a magician, however…

Ao Dan closed his eyes to his familiar living room and set up a scrying spell. It wasn't the normal spell that he'd been taught as a young wizard. It used no ingredients. Instead, he'd found that the most effective version siphoned off some of that wild chaotic magic that he was used to and sent out a stream of metaphorical fire in all directions, as well as focusing more on sound than sight.

He found the first ping directly, somewhere over to the east. He couldn't judge how far away it was, though he would say that it felt close. The sound tickled his jaw as he focused on it.

Now came the next step. Could Ao Dan create a portal, just based on that sound and position?

They'd successfully experimented in their living space, as well as taking a beacon to the far side of the colony. However, that wasn't a great enough distance, at least as far as either of them were concerned.

When Ao Dan wanted to reach Earth, he had to configure a different type of portal.

They had yet to reach that sort of distance within the colony.

The first step that evening was for Ao Dan to generate a portal in front of him. At least Henry was used to the idea of using ashes, particularly since Ao Dan was able to clean them out of the carpet magically.

Henry didn't have to know that the ashes were frequently from the cremation of creatures, some of which had been human.

Ao Dan was easily able to create a second portal based on the location of the beacon. However, the distance was still too close, and Ao Dan was able to create a normal portal there, not an altered one. He linked the two, let them run for a minute, making certain that he could transport something through them, then shut the portals down. While he knew that no mundane human would have been able to detect the anomaly, he was still too used to being hidden to ever do potentially visible magic and feel comfortable about it.

Then Ao Dan went looking for the second beacon. It, too, was basically to the east.

This time, the ringing was fainter, though still very clear.

When Ao Dan tried to create a regular portal next to the beacon, he found it wouldn't coalesce. It kept falling apart.

He would have to create a modified portal this time.

The failure excited him. They were getting someplace, now.

The third beacon was in orbit, 254 miles away.

Ao Dan wasn't sure where the space station was orbiting currently, compared to the location of the colony. He slowly searched the area around him, staying ground based, before he turned his focus upward.

It rang clearly once he passed over it, as though it were as close as the second one.

In minutes, Ao Dan had built the two portals and linked them.

It surprised him that before he could shut them off, Henry came stumbling through.

"Why did you do that?" Ao Dan scolded. Henry

appeared as though he'd been flash frozen, coming across the distance unprotected by a suit.

"I had to try it," Henry whispered, clinging to Ao Dan and sharing his cold. "I had to walk through the abyss itself."

Ao Dan shuddered as much from the cold as from the realization that Henry was never going to recover from this experience. He was never going to get his giggling, happy lover back.

He was going to reach the stars, though. Maybe that would be enough.

"Now, warm me up and make love to me," Henry said, his voice cracking. "Then you'll have to send me back."

"Of course, my love," Ao Dan said, guiding his lover out of the living room and to their shared bedroom.

He didn't know how many more times he'd be able to hold Henry like this, so he tried to make every time count, despite the tears.

———

AFTER THE FIRST SUCCESSFUL EXPERIMENTS, Henry insisted that there was more tweaking he wanted to do, primarily to boost the beacon's signal and improve the distance it could be located at. They weren't sure how they were going to test that, however.

Could they send a beacon on a ship returning to Earth, calculating how far away the beacon was based on time, with Ao Dan creating test portals every hour or so? It would be a long journey, as it still took over two hundred days to reach Earth. Ao Dan knew they needed more tests, but he also suspected that they'd reached the point when he was going to have to reach out to some other magicians.

Maybe Sunny could put him in touch with someone, maybe back on Earth…

That evening, Ao Dan created a portal for Henry in the kitchen, unable to deny Henry his obsession. After all, it did seem to settle something in his soul while observing, though it was stealing away more and more of his wits.

He then left to do some of his own work, coming back after an hour or so. He'd assumed that Henry would be staring off into space as he so frequently did these days.

However, tonight, Henry stared straight at the portal on the countertop, his eyes wide. A small dribble of drool traveled down the corner of his slack mouth. Though Ao Dan kept Henry's hair trimmed short, it seemed as though the curls all stood up on top of his head, like a cartoon character who'd been electrified.

A chittering noise came from the portal itself.

Ao Dan immediately collapsed the portal, bringing Henry back to himself.

"Why'd you do that?" he said, wiping the corners of his mouth with the back of his hand.

"What was that noise?" Ao Dan asked, feeling like a teacher who'd just caught his star student cheating.

"What noise?" Henry replied, trying to sound innocent, but Ao Dan wasn't fooled.

"There was something on the other side of the portal," Ao Dan said.

Henry shrugged. "It is magic," he said. "A portal to nowhere."

Ao Dan realized his mistake. For Henry's observations, he'd generally only ever created a single portal, that indeed, went nowhere. He never bothered linking a second portal, or specifying a place for the first one to go.

He cursed his own inattention, though he suspected that it wasn't all his fault. This had the sticky fingers of Sunny all over it.

"You've observed enough tonight," Ao Dan said.

Henry's jaw grew stubborn. "You just don't want me to take away your specialness. What would happen if I could replicate everything you do through science? Took away your magic?"

Ao Dan surprised both of them by laughing. "Be my guest," he said. If anyone could do it, it would have to be someone like Henry, whose grip on reality was already shaky.

That would sure take the fire out of *Huli* Transport, if the magicians and messengers they trained could be replaced with computers and machines.

Henry collapsed back in on himself. "I keep trying," he whispered, wrapping his arms across his chest and hugging himself, as if the cold of the portal had suddenly enfolded him. "But there are lines I can't seem to cross."

Ao Dan nodded. "You're just tired. You'll get there," he lied.

After he tucked Henry into their shared bed, and his love was soundly sleeping, Ao Dan considered his options.

Henry could possibly further the study of physics and magic, find more of the space where the two circles overlapped. Or he might be at the end of his abilities, falling further into madness even though he thought he was still making progress.

The chittering bothered Ao Dan. He knew of the types of demons and other unnatural creatures who existed in the space that portals bored through. Whenever he sent something or someone through a portal, he always had to be careful that a hitchhiker didn't also appear, attracted both to the power, as well as the potential to escape onto the human plane.

How long had those sorts of creatures been talking to Henry? Or had they been there all along, inspiring him? Ao Dan had no way of knowing.

What he did know was that Henry was nearing an end.

Ao Dan acknowledged that he was responsible for Henry's demise, and that he'd carry it with him to the end of his very, very long life.

Just as he was reaching the end of what he could do alone.

He needed another magician. Possibly more than one, whom he could work with to refine the portals and improve the great distances that man would now be able to travel along.

He'd been granted his greatest wish. With some additional refinements, man would now be able to reach the stars. Between Henry and Ao Dan, they'd invented the building blocks for true interstellar travel.

But Ao Dan needed help. As well as more resources than he had under his control, even with Sunny's help.

In the morning, he'd put in for medical leave, for both him and Henry. The pair of them would travel back to Earth. Ao Dan would see to it that Henry was cared for, for the rest of his days, however long that might be. And he'd make sure that Henry received credit as the inventor of the portal beacons and the first steps toward an intergalactic society.

He'd also contact *Huli* Transport, see if they could arrange at least a temporary peace between them while they built the future, and dragged along the rest of mankind, kicking and screaming.

TWO
THE SEEKER

KAN LI SAT FUMING on her side of the conference table. She couldn't believe the bullshit she was being forced to listen to.

The room was on the top floor of the San Francisco *Huli* Transport offices, in Chinatown, looking out over the busy city thirty stories below. The bay glittered in the distance, a dirty gray line on the horizon. Drones and other small aircraft darting through the air kept drawing her attention, when she needed to be focused on the men in front of her: Fu Rui, from the board of directors of *Huli* Transport, as well as this other creature.

This Ao Dan.

He was an effeminate Chinese-American man dressed in the most garish red-silk pantsuit she'd ever seen. Her eyes were going to start bleeding that color if she had to keep staring at it. He'd probably done it on purpose, just to offend her as well as everyone else in the office. He moved slowly, heavily, as if he was still getting used to Earth's gravity having just come from the Mars colony. Only one side of his black hair was growing out, the other still shaved close to his skull, like some wannabe bad boy.

Instead of presenting himself as *all that*, if he wanted to be taken seriously, he should be wearing a nice black suit and white shirt, similar to what Kan Li wore. Proper office attire. She was proud of the small logo of the company stitched to the front left pocket, the tiny fox that represented *Huli* Transport.

This *warlock* was the opposite of everything she stood for.

Oath breaker. Dealer in wild, chaotic magic. Ignorant of the most basic of rules.

As a wizard, she was offended to even have to be in the same room with him.

Why hadn't her superiors just killed Ao Dan and taken the prize he offered? She was certain that if they'd just thought it through, they would have found any number of ways to tHenry or cheat the man.

However, when men were in charge, they were rarely that clever.

Now, the company had to work with him. *She* was being paired with him.

At least he was openly out and gay, so she wouldn't have to put up with him hitting on her in addition to everything else.

"You understand the need for secrecy?" Fu Rui asked as Ao Dan finished outlining the project, talking about the beacons and how they were to be used to build distant magical portals in space.

"I do," Kan Li replied serenely, even smiling at both men, keeping her anger buried deep inside her, a tHenry she'd learned at her mama's knee. Those lessons had served her well over her thirty some years.

The only good thing about being assigned to work with this asshole was that it had brought her to the attention of the board of directors of *Huli* Transport. Fu Rui had traveled from mainland China itself to attend this meeting.

She'd never thought before about how odd it was to have mundanes on the board, but Fu Rui was about as non-magical as they got. He wore the most exquisite suit, radiating wealth and power, but he had no charms on him, nothing enchanted. Then again, there was a huge mundane shipping and distribution side of the company that she rarely dealt with.

"Once word gets out, and hopefully that won't occur until we make a formal announcement, we need to be able to present a complete solution to the governments of the world," Fu Rui said. "We need to make this work."

Kan Li could almost see the dollar signs dancing before his eyes at the thought of how much money *Huli* Transport could charge for being able to give mankind the stars. The monopoly they'd have.

And she'd be part of it. Coming in on the ground floor. It wasn't how she'd imagined that she'd get herself a corner office on the top floor, but she could see the path clearly now.

"Any questions?" Fu Rui asked as the meeting drew to a close.

"None, sir," Kan Li said, proud of how professional she sounded despite her abhorrence of her new "partner."

"Very good," Fu Rui said. He slipped a card out of the front pocket of his suit. "This is my personal card," he said.

Kan Li tried to act unimpressed, but she knew that her eyes still widened slightly.

"Call me at that number day or night if anything urgent comes up," he added.

"Thank you," Kan Li said, bowing her head as she picked up the card and slid it into her jacket pocket. Having one of the board of directors at her beck and call was just about as good as it got.

She was disappointed that she couldn't brag to anyone about it. Still, there was a chance that some of the other wizards would notice who she'd been in a meeting with that morning.

"Then I'll leave the pair of you to it," Fu Rui said, standing.

Kan Li stood as well. Ao Dan rudely stayed seated rather than showing the respect he should have.

Maybe once he'd taught Kan Li what she needed to know, she should kill him anyway. It would be an honor to remove such an enemy to the company.

She would have to consider her options.

"I wish you both the best of luck in this momentous venture. You represent not just the future of the company, but all of mankind," Fu Rui said, bowing to both of them.

Kan Li bowed deeply in return, noting that once again, Ao Dan couldn't be bothered with even the simplest of niceties.

No matter. She would deal with him after she'd sucked out every ounce of knowledge that she could get from the man.

After Fu Rui left the room, Kan Li turned back to Ao Dan.

"Shall we begin?" she asked, sweetness and light. Sugar wouldn't melt in her mouth.

"Sit," Ao Dan said with a negligent wave of his hand.

Oh yes. She could already taste his eventual demise. As well as the praise she was sure to get from her superiors once she'd completed her task.

KAN LI WATCHED, unimpressed, as Ao Dan filled the tea cup in front of him with fragrant jasmine tea.

Magic was all about transformations, calling like to like, turning a rock into a wall or a drop of water into a river. His teacup had been filled once, so the inside of it was already moist. It was an easy enough tHenry to refill it with tea.

What made her uneasy was that she was certain he'd done it using wild magic, not the ordered kind. She could smell the difference, a touch of smoke that remained in the air, as if she'd just walked through one of those stupid clouds caused by idiot vapers.

Ao Dan raised a single eyebrow, looking deliberately at her cup, then up at her face.

Kan Li rolled her eyes and did the same tHenry, though she went for a nicely roasted dark coffee with cream and a touch of honey.

"Good," Ao Dan said, as if he'd been grading her or something.

How dare he. Yet again, he was a man. Of course he felt it was his place to judge her.

Ao Dan paused, then continued. "You are going to have to learn how to find distant beacons, in places that you've never been to. I've tried working with other magicians on this. Most of them failed."

Kan Li nodded. That information had been included in the initial briefing. She didn't reply with, *That's what you get for dealing with warlocks*, though given his expression, Ao Dan had possibly heard her taunt anyway.

"I had assumed that any magician worth his or her salt would be able to automatically find a beacon, once they'd been exposed to the sound. However, it appears that fewer are sensitive to it than I'd hoped." He sighed, sounding frustrated. "The company explained to me why you're here, why you've been recommended. I need you to convince me why I should bother working with you."

Kan Li kept a smile on her face despite the implied insult. "Of course!" she said brightly. "It's because of the holograms."

Ao Dan made a circling motion with his finger to get her to continue.

"I'm one of the few—possibly the only currently working wizard—who can generate a portal having only visited a place using a hologram, and not going there personally." Kan Li didn't bother to hide her pride.

Holograms were one of the ways that *Huli* Transport used to measure the strength of a wizard. They would create a classroom for messengers in training, where some of the students were real and the others were just holograms.

The sooner that a messenger noticed the holograms, the stronger he or she was assumed to be and the more magic they were thought to have.

Kan Li had taken the longest of any messenger to notice the difference. It had been tough, going through the rest of the training with that stain on her record. She'd had to fight tooth and claw just to get considered for higher training, to move beyond being a messenger and become a wizard.

She'd finally figured out how to turn that blemish into a star, though. She'd started working constantly with holograms until she got good enough to place a portal in the real location that a hologram displayed. She couldn't do it every time, maybe only one time in four. But she was working hard on raising her consistency.

Ao Dan nodded. "Were the portal any different?" he asked. "The ones based on hologram images rather than personal experience?"

"Of course not!" Kan Li said automatically.

Ao Dan shook his head at her, as if dealing with a

recalcitrant student. "You shouldn't lie to me. Not if we're going to work together."

Kan Li bit her lips together instead of answering immediately. She didn't want to admit to being different than any other wizard.

Being different was bad. She'd learned that early on as well. She'd always strived to fit in with everyone else, to only stand out based on her excellence and nothing else.

Plus, she'd told herself that she was imagining things. She hadn't actually changed the portal spell. It still felt…odd, in a way she couldn't really put her finger on.

"Do the portals feel different?" Ao Dan pressed. "When you create one based on a hologram?"

"Maybe," Kan Li admitted. "It's hard to quantify," she added hastily.

"That's good enough for now," Ao Dan said. "But in the future, when you start to feel that you're doing something different, you've got to remember that's good."

"Of course, sir," Kan Li said, nodding as if she'd just received an important lesson from a wise teacher.

She could be as different as she needed to be in order to be successful in this project.

Then Ao Dan would see just how far his student had outgrown him.

Just before she finished him off.

HULI TRANSPORT only had offices on the top five floors of the building. Executive offices were on the highest floor, with wizards taking up both floors below them, the labs down one level, and the messengers one floor below that.

Kan Li had rarely visited any of the laboratories on the twenty-seventh floor before. She'd vaguely known that it existed as a work/practice space for wizards. Instead of having smart walls that you could move and shape into the proper configuration, the walls were either permanent or constructed out of screens.

It was like stepping back into her grandmother's apartment, down in Daly City, where everything was controlled mechanically instead of electronically. A place that Kan Li had happily escaped from.

However, as electronics and magic were frequently at odds with one another, it made sense that a lab might be configured this way.

One part of the floor was dedicated to making mechanical time pieces, the sort that messengers used when a portal could only be maintained for a short while. These were particularly useful if the messenger was visiting one of the planes an immortal or a god had carved out. Human electronics wouldn't work in those areas.

They passed by the watchmakers, down a long hallway past several doors to the very end. A young earnest-looking Asian man sat on a tall stool beside the door, reading, like a bouncer for a nerdy book club. He wore a plain black suit and white shirt, though the material wasn't as high quality as Kan Li's, nor did it fit him well. He looked younger than Kan Li, probably in his late teens, with wide set eyes that gave him an innocent look.

Kan Li assumed that he must be someone's relation to rate such a cushy job. While merit occasionally drove promotions in *Huli* Transport corporation—particularly among the wizards and messengers—a lot of the managers didn't have that much magic. They didn't need it for the job they did. Magical abilities only ran in families about half the time, so when a son or daughter did turn out to be magical, their path was practically guaranteed.

The guard stood up as they approached. Kan Li was

surprised at the amount of power that suddenly spiked through the air. The young man evidently took his guard duties seriously. Or possibly that was why he'd been given the job in the first place.

Kan Li doubted that the young man could wield that much power effectively. Then again, a sledgehammer was probably a better tool than a lockpick in this situation, knocking out or killing any intruders. The powerful curtain of power made Kan Li's skin buzz, like the sonics coming from a particularly raucous club. Not that she'd ever go to such a place on her own, but only when her roommate had bribed her.

Both Ao Dan and Kan Li showed the guard their badges. He verified them with a quick spell before he keyed open the scanner set beside the door.

Ao Dan placed his hand on the scanner first. The machine acknowledged that it was he. Kan Li did the same before the door slid open.

The guard had already gone back to his book by the time they stepped through the door.

The hallway they stepped into seemed identical to the one they'd just walked through, with permanent walls and lighting actually coming from bulbs recessed into the ceiling. Ao Dan laughed quietly and reached out, sliding his fingers across one of the beige walls.

Colors bloomed as his hand passed, a riotous jungle of trees, vines, and flowers.

Kan Li was so shocked at his disrespect that she paused for a moment, not moving again until Ao Dan looked over his shoulder at her, grinning, daring her to do something.

How dare he violate company property like that? It just wasn't right.

He wasn't right.

But she didn't waste the energy turning the walls back to

beige. It wasn't the time to confront Ao Dan. Not until later, when she already had stuck a knife into his ribs.

They walked a short distance to the end of the hallway and up to another door. This time, the scanner port was open. They both reaffirmed their identity before the locked door in front of them clicked open.

Kan Li wasn't sure what to expect when she walked in. It certain wasn't two short poles, each about three feet high, each sticking out of a base about three feet across. They looked like steel stanchions, the kind used at fancy concert halls. All that was missing was the red velvet rope between them, barring access.

The rest of the room was bare of ornaments. Plain white walls, a six-foot-long worktable shoved into one corner, a counter to the right of the door with a data pad sitting on it. Old-fashioned panels made up the ceiling, with fluorescent lights behind them. Vinyl tiles covered the floor, in a random pattern of light brown and cream, reminding Kan Li of her grandmother's bathroom.

"These are the beacons," Ao Dan announced proudly. "The one on the right is an original. The other was created by scientists here."

Now that Kan Li looked closer, she could see that the one on the right looked more dinged up, the surface scratched.

Kan Li had been expecting more of a black box. "So how do they work?" she asked, politely staying where she was next to the door.

Ao Dan shook his head. "I don't understand the physics of it. There aren't many who do. But somehow, my insane husband managed to cross the line between the magical and the mundane."

Kan Li hadn't really believed that when she'd heard it during the briefing. No mere mortal should have been able to create something that worked for or on someone who had magic. The two belonged in completely separate worlds.

Of course, the damned chaos magician and his supposedly insane husband wanted to break all those rules.

Ao Dan reached for a button that had been sitting behind the data pad, out of sight. It was a small round base with a rubber center.

Nothing happened when Ao Dan pressed the button.

He peered at her intently.

"Did you feel that?" he asked, sounding disappointed.

Kan Li shook her head. Damn it. She was not going to fail.

She strode farther into the room, placing herself directly in front of the two beacons. "Try it again."

"I get a tingling feeling along my jaw when the beacon pings," Ao Dan said. He reached up and rubbed at the spot, as if it itched.

Kan Li focused on Ao Dan for a moment. It occurred to her that his magical battery, as it were, was probably contained in that bright gold earring he wore.

Most magicians had a charmed item that they constantly wore. It contained additional energy they could draw on if necessary.

She pulled back the left sleeve of her jacket, then unbuttoned the cuff of her shirt, exposing the beautiful set of prayer beads that she wore around her wrist. They'd been carved out of white jade and strung together with a bright red string.

Kan Li used the bracelet as her magical battery. The white jade held a tremendous amount of power. She didn't call on it that often, but when she did, she was always glad she had so much energy on tap.

After taking a deep breath to steady herself, Kan Li reached out with her left hand, wrapping it around the newer of the two stanchions. The metal warmed almost immediately under her fingers.

"Try it again," she said.

Ao Dan looked puzzled, but he pressed the button again.

The slightest tingling feeling raced up Kan Li's arm, as though just a whisper of a breeze had floated across her skin.

She nodded to Ao Dan, who pressed the button a third time.

Kan Li focused inward, seeking the elusive signal. It felt like searching for a ghost hiding in an empty room. Every time she thought she had it cornered, it would disappear, only to haunt her from a different corner.

She *had* to do this. Had to wipe that smug smile off Ao Dan's face. Had to prove, once again, that she was better, stronger, more capable than any of her peers.

She opened her eyes and shook her arm, feeling the prayer beads sliding around her wrist. Then she stepped closer, placing the beads directly in contact with the metal of the beacon.

Surprisingly, she felt less breeze that time, as if the ghost was intent on returning to its grave without ever sharing its secrets with her.

"Take the bracelet off," Ao Dan suggested.

"What?" Kan Li said. "Why?"

"It's interfering."

Kan Li opened her mouth then shut it again. What did a stupid warlock know about power? Even though, by all accounts, he'd been a powerful wizard before he'd broken all his oaths.

But she listened to him, just so she could prove him wrong. She slowly unwound the bracelet from her arm and place it reverently on the counter beside the door.

She couldn't believe how naked she felt without it. She'd worn it constantly for the last decade.

Still, she gamely went back and reached out to touch the stanchion again.

This time, she felt the tingling go all the way from her hand up her arm to her shoulder. She could even see the chicken flesh raised up across her flesh.

What did that mean? That she could only feel the beacon when she laid aside her most powerful artifact?

This didn't bode well for her future.

The gleam in Ao Dan's eye didn't bode well for anyone.

THEY SPENT most of the afternoon improving Kan Li's sensitivity to the pinging beacons, until she could walk all the way up the hallway to the elevators and still feel the sharp tingling.

When she walked back into the room, triumphant, Ao Dan merely nodded at her. "Good," he said. "We'll start with the scrying spells tomorrow."

Kan Li blinked, surprised that Ao Dan wanted to call off their training so early. Shouldn't they continue working through dinnertime? That was normal, after all.

"All right," Kan Li said, picking up her prayer beads off the counter. They felt heavier than she'd expected. Icy cold stabbed her skin as she wrapped them around her wrist, though the beads quickly warmed.

What the hell?

Ao Dan looked around the room with distaste. "I suppose we'll meet here again. I'll arrange for one of the beacons to be moved to another location in the building. Are there any floors that you haven't gone to?"

"Today was the first day I was on the top floor," Kan Li said.

Ao Dan gave her a wicked grin. "Good. I'll make sure that it's in some important boss's corner office."

Kan Li couldn't help but roll her eyes. Of course, he'd want to disrupt as much ongoing business as he could.

They walked silently to the elevators. Kan Li debated with herself about inviting Ao Dan out for dinner or drinks. Surely that would be expected of her if Ao Dan were a visiting wizard.

But he was a warlock. His immunity from persecution was only temporary. It wouldn't do for her to get too close to him.

She pressed both the up button as well as the down button for the elevator. He would be leaving the building, going down to street level, while she had the excuse of going back to her desk.

He didn't say anything, merely nodded at her assumption, getting onto the descending elevator without another word.

Kan Li found herself taking a deep breath once he'd left. Now, her life could get back to normal. Or at least as normal as things could be when she wasn't working on a top-secret project to give the stars to humanity.

KAN LI WAS surprised when a cheery voice greeted her as she opened the door to her shared apartment.

"Hey there!"

Pei Shan, her roommate, popped her head up over the back of the couch. She wore comfortable staying-in clothes, a pair of faded PJ bottoms with spaceships zooming across the flannel and a loose T-shirt. Her long black hair was done up in a messy bun, and her face was freshly washed.

The large screen set into the wall of the living room had a

popular anime show, though the sound had been turned off and a scrolling line of Japanese *katakana* subtitles ran across the bottom.

Pei Shan was only twenty-five and also worked at *Huli* Transport, though not as a wizard but as a messenger. She was not that powerful a magician. However, she planned on becoming one of the managers, and so spent her time working on her superpower: languages. She already spoke Mandarin, Cantonese, and Taiwanese, as well as English, French, German, and Spanish. Now, she was picking up Japanese.

Huli Transport delivered messages and packages to the gods and heroes of many different pantheons. Since it had expanded internationally, someone who could speak several languages would be an asset to any office.

"So tell me all about it!" Pei Shan said as she clicked off the screen and bounded over to Kan Li.

"All about what?" Kan Li asked as she handed her roommate her shopping bag and shrugged off her coat. She thought furiously. What lie could she tell Pei Shan?

"You went up to the top floor today," Pei Shan said over her shoulder as she walked through the hallway and into the kitchen, placing the two bags onto the little island. "Who did you meet with? Are you getting another promotion?"

Kan Li slowly hung up her jacket next to the door as she thought, then bravely walked into the kitchen. "I can't tell you the details," she said, settling on the truth.

Pei Shan rolled her eyes. "Sure, sure. You can't tell *other* people the details. I don't count."

Kan Li couldn't help but giggle. Though Pei Shan drove her crazy sometimes with her, well, exuberance for want of a better term, the reason why Kan Li never actually kicked her out was because Pei Shan could always make her laugh.

Even the one time when Kan Li had accidently killed a

messenger because a damned demon had hitchhiked a ride on the portal she'd opened.

"This time, I can't tell you," Kan Li said, walking over to where her roommate stood. "I really can't."

Kan Li knew her roommate too well. She knew that Pei Shan would never be able to keep a secret as big as this. She'd blurt it out the next time she got overly excited. It was a wonder she'd managed to stay employed this long as a messenger.

"Not even if I pinky swear never to tell another soul?" Pei Shan asked, batting her eyes at Kan Li.

"Not even then," Kan Li said heavily. "But I will tell you when I can," she promised.

"Deal!" Pei Shan said brightly. "Now, what did you bring me to eat?"

"What if I told you I'd only gotten enough for me?" Kan Li teased as she opened the first bag.

"I'd call you a selfish old thing who should know better."

Kan Li giggled again. She did know better, and so had ordered two of her favorite dishes from the Chinese takeout place down the street. That way, they'd both have leftovers for tomorrow.

The heavenly smell of fried rice and vat-grown shrimp rose up from one carton, while the other contained a fabulous egg foo yung with a sharp brown sauce.

When they'd both settled onto the couch with their cartons and their chopsticks, Kan Li asked, "Weren't you supposed to be gone tonight? Didn't you have a date?"

Pei Shan gave an exaggerated sigh. "I was. He canceled. Again."

"I'm sorry," Kan Li said. No wonder Pei Shan had settled in for the evening, wearing her most comfortable clothes while still studying.

Though *Huli* Transport was a traditional Chinese

company, with all the traditional male chauvinism that went along with it, the culture had to change due to the ancient policy of "one couple, one child" that the mainland had enforced long ago.

Too many male children had been born, while the female children had either been given away or aborted. Though it had taken a long time, all Chinese companies now accepted that females had to be on boards and in power if they wanted to survive.

Some of the ancient attitudes still prevailed despite it being the year 2208, but the laws had all been changed. Even as little as a generation before, Pei Shan's primary path for getting ahead would have been to marry well.

Now, she really could build her own career, her own way, with little interference.

"So what can you tell me about the new project you're working on?" Pei Shan asked after a while.

Kan Li thought for a moment. "Well, you'll probably see me at some point with that damned warlock. Ao Dan," she said. If nothing else, other people in the company were sure to see her in the elevator with him, getting off on the same floor.

Pei Shan's eyes widened. "Really?" she sighed. "Is he as tragic as they say?"

"Huh?" Kan Li asked, confused. Ao Dan? Tragic? What the hell?

"His current husband is insane," Pei Shan confided. "Henry. They both showed up in the company offices a month ago or so, going to the labs. Henry started babbling and drooling in the elevator. Ao Dan just kept talking to him the entire time, trying to bring him back to reality. It was supposedly heartbreaking."

Kan Li nodded. Ao Dan had casually mentioned that his husband was insane. She hadn't thought it was the literal truth, though. "What do you think happened to him?" Surely Ao Dan wasn't so chaotic that he married the other man because he was insane, right?

"No one knows," Pei Shan said. "Maybe his genes weren't clean."

"Or more likely, being so exposed to chaos magic drove him crazy," Kan Li said.

Pei Shan opened her mouth, then shut it again, shaking her head.

"What?" Kan Li asked.

"Too much law isn't good either," Pei Shan said.

Kan Li sighed. "I know. You've said more than once that I need to loosen up and live a little. But I'm afraid." Kan Li blinked, surprised at herself. She generally wasn't this honest.

"What are you afraid of?" Pei Shan asked gently.

"Afraid of going back," Kan Li said all in a rush. "Afraid of being stuck like my mother and my grandmother." Stuck in loveless marriages because it was the only way out of their situation. Stuck with husbands who flaunted their mistresses. Stuck in the past and in old ways that no longer worked in modern America.

"You won't," Pei Shan said, reaching out and taking Kan Li's hand in hers, squeezing it tightly. "You're too stubborn to be dragged backwards. You'll only move forward. I know it."

Kan Li held onto her roommate's hand for a moment before letting it go. She took another bite of egg foo young while she considered her past, her present, her future.

Must have been spending all afternoon with such an ancient old man that had gotten her shaken up this way. And Ao Dan truly was ancient. Two hundred and fifty years old by all accounts. He used archaic language and terms, and had reminded her too strongly of her grandfather.

With gene screening, selection, and the right treatments, only the top echelons of humanity had access to that sort of long life. And the record for the oldest mundane person was still only one hundred and sixty.

But what if moving forward meant being different? Standing out from everyone else?

Kan Li still wasn't sure she wanted to make that leap.

THE SAME YOUNG man sat on the stool outside the locked corridor on the lab floor, wearing either the same suit or something similar enough. He took her ID and scrutinized it, casting a small spell to ensure its authenticity, before he keyed open the scanner set beside the door.

Though Kan Li hadn't been paying that much attention, she would swear that the code was different today than yesterday. It might have changed halfway through the afternoon as well.

Seemed they really were taking their security seriously.

The riot of colors in the hallway shocked her as much today as they had the day before. She was tempted to attack them, erase them all, make them fade back to a nice, soothing beige.

Something stayed her hand, though. She wasn't sure what. Maybe she would need that shock every morning to remind her that she must do something *different* this time, if she wanted to succeed.

What was that old definition of insanity? Trying the exact same thing and expecting different results?

Of course, Ao Dan wasn't there at the start of work. He'd probably not come strolling in until midmorning.

Only one of the beacons still stood in the room. The other had probably been transported to some poor executive's office.

Fine. She could start without Ao Dan here. Practice some more.

Kan Li hesitated, then she pushed back the sleeve on her suit jacket and unbuttoned the cuff on her shirt. She shook her wrist, the white jade prayer beads sliding across her skin.

Why had they felt so cold when she put them on yesterday afternoon? Why had it almost hurt?

She still didn't know. She'd tried to ask Pei Shen in oblique terms if she'd ever heard of such a thing, but she hadn't gotten a satisfactory answer.

Instead of worrying about it, Kan Li merely unwound the bracelet and put it on the counter again before she reached for the button that would activate the beacon in front of her.

This morning, she heard the pinging sound right away. With her eyes closed, Kan Li tried one of the exercises Ao Dan had made her do the day before: close her eyes and spin around, then try to pinpoint the beacon.

She spun around a few times, making herself dizzy, before she pressed the button again.

Wait. Were there two sounds?

No. Just the one off to her left.

Kan Li oriented herself in the direction she felt certain the beacon stood before she opened her eyes.

Ao Dan had also appeared, standing just beyond the beacon.

"Good," he said, nodding in approval. "You've grown more sensitive to the sound of the beacon. Now, you need to find the one that's hidden."

Kan Li nodded, pleased. She could do this. She would show this man, show them all, that she was never about to go back.

THE SPELL that Ao Dan taught Kan Li for scrying and finding the other beacon was different than the one she normally would use. It felt weird doing such a spell with no ingredients. Normally, she'd have to use at the very least some pulverized crystal powder and maybe some ivy leaves.

Instead, Ao Dan started off with a chant of nonsense words, meant to focus his attention. Couldn't the man at least translate them into Mandarin or something?

Kan Li found herself getting more and more angry the longer Ao Dan chanted. He wore a purple jumpsuit that day. The color really didn't suit him—made his skin looked washed out. His face was puffy as well, as if he hadn't been sleeping.

There was something wrong with him, and not just because he was a chaos magician.

However, when Ao Dan finally got on with the spell, Kan Li *felt* the stream of fire the man emitted, going out in all directions. It had that burnt smell of wild magic, and raised the hairs up along the back of her neck.

"You don't expect me to use that spell, do you?" Kan Li asked. As Ao Dan was generally deliberately rude, she'd decided to match him that day, to give him a taste of his own behavior.

Ao Dan merely raised a single eyebrow at her. "I do," he said. "It's the most effective way of finding the beacons."

Kan Li shook her head. "There has *got* to be another way! Or is that part of your plan? To turn all regular wizards into worshippers of chaos?"

Ao Dan rolled his eyes at her. "My so-called *master plan* is to get us off this damned planet so that we'll have a chance at actually living instead of blowing each other up."

Kan Li huffed at him, though she suspected he was being truthful with her.

She was sensitive to the beacons. She'd proven that

yesterday, as well as that morning. She could find them when they were nearby, feel their ping.

She would be able to find them with a spell as well.

Just not that spell.

Kan Li had never crafted a spell from scratch before. But if that was what it took, so be it.

"Tell me what you feel when you're scrying," she said, peering at Ao Dan.

"With the normal spell? Besides feeling like a peeping Tom?" Ao Dan asked.

"No," Kan Li said. "Using the beacon-finding spell. What does it feel like?"

"There's a fire that goes with it," Ao Dan replied slowly. "Like a beam."

Kan Li nodded. That would be the chaotic, wild magic that Ao Dan called on. She'd felt that as well.

However, if she wanted to keep her soul, she would have to find a different spell. She did *not* want to touch the chaotic magic as Ao Dan had.

She would just have to use her own fire, instead.

Mama had always taught Kan Li to keep her anger locked deep inside of herself, to put on a smile for the world to see. Never to show too much.

However, Mama had never asked Kan Li to not have those feelings, that anger. In her own way, Mama had encouraged Kan Li to keep that fire burning. So it had never been smothered, just banked, white hot.

Until now.

Kan Li closed her eyes and touched that sore spot, the hurts that would never go away. How she'd been overlooked for being a woman, for having a grandmother who hadn't been Chinese as her family wasn't rich enough, didn't have the connections in order to breed true as they overcame the idiocy of the former government policies.

It wasn't right. It wasn't fair.

It had been the hand she'd been dealt.

Kan Li wasn't sure how to siphon off just a little of that burning rage. No matter. She could refine the spell later, tune it down into a beam instead of an ever-expanding disk of rage.

It took her two seconds to find the beacon stashed just a few floors up. Two more seconds to build a portal there.

Once released, though, her fury wouldn't be denied. She couldn't pull it back.

And truthfully, she really didn't want to.

Her awareness went out and up. Past the building. Beyond the San Francisco Bay. Up. Out.

There was a sound she followed there, something she hadn't been expecting. Something she'd never felt before. It was the faintest of trails, like specks of glitter left behind after the party had been cleaned up.

Still up. Still out. Past the atmosphere. Out to the stars.

She could get there, wherever that *there* was. She knew it existed. She just had to find it.

Up. Out.

She *would* get there. She would show them all. And damn anyone who said she couldn't.

The further Kan Li cast the spell out from her physical body, the more her focus narrowed. She felt as though she was surfing on top of an ever-cresting wave that no longer went in every direction but just one. West was the direction she'd call it, though she really didn't have a sense of location.

Just outward. Onward. Toward that bell-like tone she could barely make out in the distance, growing louder all the time.

The sound both annoyed her as well as soothed her. She *had* to find it. Had to get a lock on it, like those silly heat-seeking drones that the boys on her block had played with, divebombing her as she walked home alone from school.

There it was. She felt the tall tower the sound echoed from, though she knew it wasn't that tall, just a portal beacon, maybe four feet in height. There was something about the shape though, when located at a distance, that made it as tall as a lighthouse in her head.

Just getting a lock on it wasn't enough. Could she place herself there? Create a portal? As she had for the holograms?

The part Kan Li hadn't told Ao Dan about, hadn't told anyone about, was how the hologram portals always felt more personal. The other portals she created were outside, external to her. They were a separate door that she built and sent messengers through.

She always felt more attached to the hologram portals, as if threads of magic stayed tied to her wrists and ankles, tangled in her hair. It was almost as if an essential part of her soul was woven into the hologram portals.

The other difference was that she never drew on the battery of power from her prayer beads to create those types of portals. No, she only drew from a well of strength deep inside herself.

The beacon portal felt the same way. As with the rage, the magic to fuel the portal came from inside of her alone, and connected her to it in a way that she could never fully explain.

It wasn't a birth, but it was a creation that came from deep inside her soul. All the other portals were interchangeable. These weren't. Possibly if a wizard had the right training, they'd be able to identify the creator of the portal and track it back to her.

When Kan Li opened her eyes, she felt gratified by the shock and surprise on Ao Dan's face.

"You reached the beacon on Mars, didn't you? And created a portal there!" he said. "How?"

Kan Li merely smirked. "Wasn't that what I was supposed to do?"

"It was," Ao Dan said. He peered at her closely, as if seeing her for the first time. "You will have to teach me, and others, how to do it."

Kan Li nodded. Of course, the consequences of her success would require more responsibilities. That was always the case. She stood up straighter. She was ready.

Ao Dan gave her a sudden smile. "Now, we just have to find you a partner."

"What do you mean?" Kan Li said, confused.

"Where does that portal on the Mars space station lead to?" Ao Dan asked.

Kan Li felt for the portal, the soft blue and gray oval with the black abyss contained within. That blackness should go somewhere. She'd assumed that it would automatically connect to the portal in the office upstairs.

How did one create a portal that didn't go anywhere? She hadn't meant to do that!

She double-checked.

The one upstairs didn't go anywhere either.

Ao Dan nodded at her, as if she'd been speaking her thoughts out loud. "You may, you may not, be able to link the two portals. What I've found is that the further the distance, the more magic it takes to join the opening and closing portals together. The only times I had any success was when I had two magicians working together: one to create the distant portal, and a second to create and hold the closer of the two. Then either one or the other of us could link them."

"I see," Kan Li said. She tried to keep her spirits buoyed up.

Of course, she couldn't have this victory all to herself. She was going to have to continue to work as a team. Her mother would be proud of her achievement, and as equally proud that her daughter's work was going to undo some of that American individualism that she'd felt had corrupted her daughter, replacing it with a proper sense of belonging.

Kan Li would not despair. She'd done something miraculous that day. Found a beacon on Mars and planted her portal there.

Even if the future meant more teams and groups.

KAN LI RELEASED the portal on the Mars space station with regret. It felt like burning a poem that she'd spent weeks crafting, even though the characters had been written on the back of a fading leaf.

She felt spent when she let it go, as exhausted as she'd felt when she'd first started training as a wizard.

Ao Dan and Kan Li had little success that afternoon linking any portal from Earth to Mars. Despite Ao Dan creating what appeared to Kan Li as a normal portal, using ash to ground it and calling burning characters out of the air one by one, it was still different. The portal didn't feel right to her. The inky blackness in the center of the swirling gray was colder than it should have been, eating at her soul.

And Kan Li had learned to her chagrin that she was incapable of linking two portals together when they were at such an incredible distance apart.

No, they were going to have to find another wizard to generate the portals here on Earth, someone who Kan Li could work with.

After their last failed attempt they stood on either side of the table they'd dragged to the center of the lab, glaring at each other and sweating. The air filtration system couldn't cope with the scent of smoke and ashes, making Kan Li feel as though her lungs were filthy in addition to her hands being covered in soot.

"We've made good progress," Ao Dan said grudgingly as he stepped back from his side of the table. "But it's time to go."

Kan Li blinked, surprised, then shook her head.

Of course he wouldn't want to work through dinner. She would, given a chance, despite being both hungry and tired. It was the only thing she knew how to do—work hard, then work harder.

"Should I contact Fu Rui?" Kan Li asked. Though she hated to admit defeat, at least for the time being it made sense that they should bring in someone else.

She'd keep working at it, however. She *had* to be able to do this herself.

"I'll send him a message," Ao Dan said. "He needs to know the type of wizard to search for."

Kan Li found that since she'd tapped into that anger, it was much more difficult to push it back. The next words fell unbidden from her lips. "And what type of wizard is that?" she snapped.

Ao Dan gave her a knowing grin. "Someone who won't have their feathers ruffled easily. They also need to be very powerful. Stronger than most. They don't need a lot of specialized training. Able to create a portal, but that's about it."

"Don't they need to be sensitive to the beacons?" Kan Li asked, confused.

Ao Dan shook his head. "No, they'd don't need to be. They are the holder, the one focused on the here and now. The seeker needs to be able to find the beacons at a distance."

Kan Li thought about the arrangement for a moment, then shook her head. "Won't be enough," she said.

"What do you mean?" Ao Dan asked, confused.

"We're going to need a third. A seeker to find the distant beacon, a holder for the space here. And a pilot to navigate from one portal to the next."

Ao Dan's eyes took on a distant look. "You may be right. Though maybe ships will be able to pilot themselves," he said slowly. "It's going to be the rare wizard who can do all three tasks by himself."

Kan Li didn't automatically correct him, to use a more gender-neutral form of pronoun. He was an ancient dinosaur, after all. Probably unable to learn new tHenrys.

She suddenly remembered her vow from earlier, to bleed Ao Dan dry of information before she bled him dry with a knife.

That anger was still there. But it had tapered down some.

It was her duty to kill this chaos warlock before he infected all of the other wizards with his wild ideas.

Except that now, she wasn't sure she would be able to. Not after seeing his power, working with him so closely to get their portals aligned.

And that just made her angrier.

———

KAN LI WAITED for her roommate to get home. She'd washed her hair and put it up in a messy bun, tendrils still falling around her face. It felt good to get out of her work outfit and into comfy navy-blue flannel sweats and a T-shirt. She'd already eaten dinner—leftover pita and gyros this time —and had her feet up on the couch, thinking.

It had been a frustrating week. Kan Li hadn't been back to her desk the entire time. Instead, she'd worked with Ao

Dan on the floor with the labs, though not in the far back room, but instead, in one of the magical practice rooms.

The wizards who'd been tested only knew that the company was trying to create a different type of portal. They wouldn't be read into the project until they'd proved that they could build portals that either Ao Dan or Kan Li could link to, or that they could link to pre-built portals themselves.

Kan Li had liked to think that wizards, in general, were somewhat easy going. There were very few wizards who'd gone straight from discovering that they had magic to wizard training. Most of them had come up through the ranks, starting off as a messenger before receiving more training.

Because of her roommate, Kan Li had hung out more with the messengers than with the wizards. They were a raucous bunch. She understood why. In order to be a good messenger, you had to be willing to live on the wild side. You never knew where your next job would take you. The traditional vehicle for a messenger was still a motorcycle, though modernized, now, with an automatic transmission and stability gyros.

Plus, even though the company did everything they could to protect the messengers, they were still killed at an alarming rate. Once a human started seeing the magical side of things, monsters and other creatures would start noticing them. In addition, hitchhikers still came through portals sometimes, frequently killing not only the messenger but the wizard as well.

Kan Li had always been more conservative than the other messengers when she'd been one herself. But she'd prided herself on still being able to hang out with them every once in a while.

The wizards she'd met that week were, well, too stuffy to

do so comfortably. It was as if their training had turned them increasingly conservative.

Kan Li had never considered herself a maveHenry. She'd always worked hard at fitting in with the group, only standing out due to excellence.

After this week, she realized just how different she actually was, and had to keep reassuring herself that was a good thing. Ao Dan had certainly said so, more than once.

There were very few wizards who could have worked with Ao Dan to start with. Even fewer who would have been willing to learn from the man.

Kan Li understood their disgust. Ao Dan represented the opposite of every law-abiding wizard. However, these fools couldn't see beyond their own noses. They had to understand that they needed to work together for the future instead.

She still thought about killing Ao Dan once the project was over. She knew that her superiors probably expected it of her.

She wasn't sure now, though. If nothing else, the other wizards needed someone like Ao Dan to show them their faults.

"Honey, I'm home!" Pei Shan called as she walked in the door.

Kan Li grinned. That had always been a joke between them as they did sometimes act like an old married couple.

"I got your message," Pei Shan said as she came into the living room. She was still dressed in her messenger leathers, brown and padded, reinforced with steel thread so she'd survive a crash, even at the speeds that Kan Li knew Pei Shan preferred. "What's so important?"

"You've heard the rumors, right?" Kan Li said as she swung her feet down from the coffee table. "About how the company is investigating building a new type of portal?"

Pei Shan nodded solemnly. "Of course, no one told me

officially," she said. "But there have been so many different wizards passing through the building this week."

Kan Li gave her a quick smile. "Yeah. Stuck up pHenrys, mostly. Including the women."

Pei Shan snorted.

"So, since I'm supposed to be working closely with whoever manages to help out on this project, I figured I'd ask you to try as well," Kan Li said. Since none of the other wizards were able to do the job, Kan Li thought she may as well try to link a portal with someone she actually liked.

"Really?" Pei Shan said. She blinked, then her posture grew stiff and she grew more solemn. "What exactly are you trying to do?"

"What I'd like to do is for you to build a portal. Just a small one. Package sized. Then I'll build one. And then see if we can link them together," Kan Li explained.

Pei Shan narrowed her eyes at Kan Li. "What do you mean, link them together? Wouldn't they already be linked?"

Kan Li kept her sigh to herself. This had been the issue with so many of the wizards to start with. They had no concept of building a portal to nowhere, when the destination would be picked out later.

"We can try building them together so that they'll automatically be linked," Kan Li said. They'd tried that several times and it had never worked. "But I'd also like you to try creating a portal that really doesn't go anywhere."

Pei Shan nodded. "And if I can do that, and you can link the portals together, then what?"

"Then I get to tell you all about what we're working on!" Kan Li said brightly, though she knew it wasn't going to be that easy. Pei Shan was mostly a messenger. She'd had a little bit of arcane training, but she just wasn't that strong a magician.

But maybe strength wasn't really what they needed. Maybe Kan Li could be strong enough for both portals.

After a few moments, Pei Shan shook her head. "I'd like to decline, if that's all right."

"What?" Kan Li said, shock striking the center of her chest like a solid blow. "Why? I don't understand."

Pei Shan sat down on the edge of the couch. "I know that your deepest desire is to be the strongest wizard alive. You don't really understand anyone who doesn't want to be a wizard, who doesn't want to grab that power with both hands. But I don't."

"You're still studying to be a manager," Kan Li pointed out. "You're trying to get power too."

Pei Shan sighed. "Just to make my life easier," she admitted. "Not because I'm driven. Not like you. Plus, I want a family. A husband. Kids."

Kan Li shook her head. "You can still have those if this works."

Pei Shan just lifted her eyebrows and stared at Kan Li. "How many wizards do you know of who are married?"

"Uhmmm," was all Kan Li could say in response.

"Exactly. I can only think of one," Pei Shan said. "Besides Ao Dan, of course."

Kan Li blinked in surprise. Ao Dan was married, wasn't he? He had driven his husband insane. But at least he had a partner.

Unlike all the wizards she knew…

"So that's it?" Kan Li said after a moment. "You won't even try because you want a family instead?"

Pei Shan gave her a sad smile. "You don't need me to try. You'll find someone. You won't stop until you do."

Kan Li had to admit that her roommate was right. She wasn't about to stop.

She just didn't understand Pei Shan's preference for family over personal power.

Then again, maybe in that way too, Kan Li was just too different from everyone else.

———

KAN LI WALKED SLOWLY down the hallway on Monday morning, going back to the room with the beacon. She and Ao Dan had agreed to try it again, just the pair of them, see if they could figure out how to build portals together and link them.

Because Kan Li would *not* be thwarted.

She'd gone back and forth all weekend when thinking about Ao Dan. Should she kill him? Shouldn't she? Should she at least wait until his husband died? Had he already infected her with chaos magic? Was that why she could work with the beacons?

The same young man sat guard at the door. He grimaced as she drew near. "More headaches?" he asked her, instead of saying good morning.

"I beg your pardon?" Kan Li asked frostily.

He seemed to suddenly realize what he'd said. He put both of his hands over his mouth as if he could hide the words. "I'm sorry. I'm sorry. I don't know why I said that. Please, please forgive me. I'm sorry."

Kan Li stood there, puzzled. "What did you mean by more headaches?"

The young man shook his head and looked at the floor instead of meeting her eye.

"Tell me," Kan Li said, more softly than she'd planned.

After heaving a great sigh, the young man finally said, "When you work in that room back there, I get a headache. Right here," he added, rubbing the base of his skull.

"All the time?" Kan Li asked sharply.

The man shrugged and finally looked up at her. "Just sometimes. It comes and goes."

"What is your name and who is your manager?" Kan Li said, putting two and two together, excitement coursing through her.

"Xi Niu," he said miserably. He named a middle-manager who Kan Li had worked with before. She called him directly, ordering him to get a replacement for Xi Niu right away.

Xi Niu looked completely dejected as they waited. Kan Li couldn't help but grin.

A tall, thin man came striding up shortly, looking as though he owned the entire world. "I am Gi Doh," he said, bowing his head. "*His* replacement."

"I see," Kan Li said. She reached out and grabbed Xi Niu's arm before he could escape. "I need Xi Niu to help me in the lab."

That appeared to take the wind out of Gi Doh's sails. "I see."

Kan Li gestured to the keypad. "Aren't you going to let us in?"

"Ah, right, sure," Gi Doh said.

Kan Li rolled her eyes as he quickly keyed open the screen. Why hadn't he checked their badges as Xi Niu had? She was really going to have to have another word with their manager.

Kan Li ignored Xi Niu's gasp at the colors that Ao Dan had painted across the walls. She practically pulled him down the hall.

Once they got into the room with the beacon, she picked up the button that activated the beacon and pressed it.

"Can you feel that?" she demanded.

Wide-eyed, Xi Niu nodded. He rubbed the back of his skull. "Yes, I can," he said.

Triumphant, Kan Li asked, "Do you have the training to build a portal?"

"I do," Xi Niu said slowly. "Though I'm new. I've only been taking wizard training for about six weeks."

Kan Li gestured for him to start. Portals were one of the first things that wizards were trained in. If they couldn't create a portal, they were frequently demoted back to messenger.

"Here? Now?"

"Here. Now. Floating and not grounded," she said, hoping that he'd understand.

Xi Niu shrugged. That incredibly strong curtain of magic rained down on her, only this time, it didn't make her skin itch.

It impressed her that he was able to build a non-grounded portal without ingredients on the first try. Though he might have claimed to be new, he certainly had some skill.

However, that he wasn't fully trained also worked in his favor. He hadn't immediately asked where the portal was supposed to go *to*. No, he just built a portal to nowhere, as she instructed.

The portal that Xi Niu built floated in midair, directly beside the beacon. The swirling blackness in the center wasn't as cold as the portals that Ao Dan built, but the gray oval held more power than any Kan Li had ever seen.

And she'd seen a lot of different portals that week.

Quickly, Kan Li built a second portal in the room, floating next to Xi Niu's. She purposefully built one that was different, that was more connected to her, like a beacon portal. "Now, we have to join these two portals. Link them together."

Xi Niu nodded. He didn't ask how or why. He just attacked the problem in front of him.

With a sledgehammer.

The power floating through the room tripled. Kan Li felt even her ponytail starting to float up off her back.

Had Xi Niu's parents known how strong their son would become when they named him "Ten Ox"? Or had that strength come later, and Xi Niu had changed his name? Despite his smaller stature, he had more power than anyone Kan Li had ever worked with.

Slowly, Xi Niu forged links of magic between the two portals, connecting them together solidly. Then he beat on the links, flattening them out, until Kan Li could practically see the solid tunnel between the two portals.

"Now what?" Xi Niu asked, stepping back and viewing his handiwork.

"Now we go into space," Ao Dan said from the door behind them.

Kan Li turned to smile triumphantly at him.

Ao Dan merely nodded at her in agreement.

She'd found their Holder. They just had to build on this base, get the portals both on Earth as well as on Mars to work together.

And then maybe she would kill Ao Dan. So that only proper wizards would take the credit for moving humankind to the stars.

Or maybe she wouldn't. She might be too busy, after all, preparing all the new classes of wizards for their newest gig: transporting ships across space, instead of just messages for the gods.

THREE

THE HOLDER

XI NIU COULDN'T BELIEVE that he was actually in space. In space! In a spaceship! Floating above the Earth!

It was a *Huli* Transport corporate spaceship, used to deliver people and goods to the space stations in orbit above Earth. He wore a light jumpsuit, in company brown and red. They weren't going to be up here for long, so he hung out in the passenger lounge, looking out the window. He held onto a handy bar right next to the window, his legs floating behind him.

He'd never seen anything like this, or felt it. Even the canned air smelled different, scented with ozone, as if a thunderstorm gathered. Sure, Xi Niu had tried the VR simulators, but like most magicians, they hadn't really worked.

Magic seemed more grounded in reality than anyone had expected, and so neither holograms nor VR worked on those who had strong magic.

And Xi Niu had more magic than most.

His parents hadn't named him "Number Ten Ox" after that character in the popular anime series. Not really. He'd actually been eight years old by the time it came out. No, they'd named him after the character in the books, *The Chronicles of Master Li*, that the series was based on. As the books were ancient, over two hundred years old, no one ever made the connection.

Xi Niu read all three books every year, on or around his birthday. He'd always wished that he were as tall or as physically strong as his namesake. His most precious possession was an actual, antique, paper version of the omnibus of the series that his uncle had given him when Xi Niu—at just nineteen—had passed the tests at *Huli* Transport and had been approved for wizard training.

Secretly, Xi Niu was kind of disappointed that he never got to be a messenger. The leathers they wore were cool looking, though he was certain he'd never look that good in them. No matter what he wore, it always seemed to look, well, slovenly. As if he were a great big ox instead of barely five foot seven inches tall with a slight build. Even his brand new jumpsuit looked wrinkled, as if he'd slept in it.

He gazed down at the blue and green planet below him. A jewel, as it had been called.

He'd never really wanted to go into space, to go live on one of the colonies. He liked Earth. He liked breathing real air and feeling the wind and actually going to the library. Yes, he read almost everything on his phone or his reader. It was still a monthly treat for him to go to a place and be surrounded by actual physical books.

His friends all told him regularly that he was never going to get a girlfriend that way.

Xi Niu hadn't minded. He wasn't really looking for a girlfriend just then. He couldn't tell them that, though.

There were a lot of things that he couldn't tell his friends about, like magic and being trained to be a wizard.

He'd only just started, and had been working at the

company for about two months, now. He'd been surprised that he'd been taken out of class and assigned guard duty that week. Then again, his manager had instructed him to use all his power if something went wrong.

Nothing had gone wrong, and Xi Niu had spent his time reading.

He hadn't made any friends at the office, not yet, not really. The rest of the wizards in his class had all started as messengers, which meant they not only knew each other, but many of the other wizards as well. He was the youngest, as well as the only outsider, in a class of eighteen.

It helped that he had a tremendous amount of magical strength. That at least made his peers vaguely respect him.

However, before Kan Li had found him and drawn him into this awesome project, he was certain that his teachers had been despairing over what to do with him.

He had all the subtlety of the ox he was named after. No finesse. Battering down a door might even be too much for him—he was more likely to blow apart the wall.

Maybe, though, just maybe, he'd found something he could do with all that strength.

He still wasn't sure why he'd told Kan Li about the headaches. Sure, it had been exactly what he'd been thinking. The words had just blurted out.

Had he been touched by one of the gods, as Ao Dan had claimed? That wouldn't be a good thing, for Sun Hou-Tse to have noticed him. Xi Niu didn't want to turn his back on everyone and become a chaos magician, to break his oaths to the company and turn into a warlock.

That just seemed like a sure path to hell.

"Xi Niu, please join us in the forward lounge," came the announcement over the speakers.

Xi Niu gave his entire body a shake. It made him grin

how he bounced around, the shimmy going from his head to his toes as he gripped the handrail harder.

He could get used to this. Or at least, regular trips into space. He would miss the Earth too much to ever relocate permanently.

But now, it was showtime.

He gave one last, long look at the planet below him, his heart both singing with joy as well as feeling powerfully melancholy. Such a sight. And he'd never be able to share it with anyone. Not even his friends could know about this trip.

He sighed, pushed himself away, then pulled himself through the open hatch and down the hallway.

Time to get into his full EVA suit.

Then…showtime.

THE FORWARD LOUNGE faced away from the Earth, looking out onto space. Large reinforced windows filled the front of the room. A big oval table stood in the center of the room, taking up most of the space. Industrial metal and leather chairs circled the table, magnetically held to the floor. It looked like a regular conference room, the kind he'd find at *Huli* headquarters.

Except for that dark view. Stars filled the sky but couldn't overcome the blackness between them.

Xi Niu didn't understand why this room had more gravity than the passenger lounge out back. It seemed like magic to him, though he knew it wasn't, that some sort of physics was involved. It wasn't Earth gravity, it was lighter. And there were handholds all along the walls, as well as on the table itself.

This room had a lot more shielding compared to the rest

of the ship. Lead lined the walls, and special paint had been applied, turning them a dark blue. Magic and electronics didn't always go together. Xi Niu had learned that quickly, having destroyed more than one phone and reader accidently. Supposedly, by only doing magic in this one room, they wouldn't blow out all the systems as well as the engines.

A second spaceship floated just beside them, out of view. If something went wrong, hopefully they'd be able to survive long enough to be rescued. But it was why they'd all put on their full EVA suits, just in case.

Xi Niu grinned at Kan Li and Ao Dan, as well as the newest addition to their team, a droll Anglo scientist named Ryan. He was taller than the rest of them, Caucasian, with blond curls that rioted across the top of his long skull, watery blue eyes, and a smile that warmed every room.

Though Xi Niu knew that Ao Dan was *ancient*, he felt younger, maybe the same age as Xi Niu's dad, in his forties or fifties. Ryan, on the other hand, had to be in his mid-seventies, and seemed to be more of an antique.

Like the others, Ryan wore a full EVA suit, in case this experiment went awry. Unlike them, though, he was mostly mundane. He had a touch of magic, just enough to see and sense the other worlds around them. But according to him, he'd failed at even the most rudimentary magical training.

Fortunately, he'd had a head for science and numbers and had been able to provide other services to the company.

Ryan held a remote-control unit in his hands. It looked primitive to Xi Niu. He was more used to using a sensory glove, particularly for flying drones. It took some skill to learn, but Xi Niu had been really good at flying the tiny machines off the rooftop of his apartment when he'd been younger.

The unit Ryan held had actual levers for directing the drone, as well as buttons for controlling its speed.

When Ryan activated the remote, a screen popped up, floating above the unit. Again, ancient tech, instead of a display that came up on either contacts or glasses. The screen was split down the middle. The right side showed what the drone saw, while the left contained all the information about the drone, showing its speed, its rotation on its center axis, and so on.

"Are you ready?" Ao Dan said, bringing Xi Niu's attention back away from the scientist.

Xi Niu merely nodded. He knew he had a job to do.

He'd practiced for about two weeks with both Ao Dan as well as Kan Li, building and linking portals together. It was easier for him to link to Kan Li's portals, though he had the sense that the ones he built with Ao Dan were stronger in some undefinable way, as though they'd last longer.

Today was a big test. They were going to try to build two portals in space, then drive a drone through them.

Xi Niu studied the space just outside the window. Where should he build the portal? There was a lot of area out there.

Then he saw the blinking lights of the drone sitting right outside of the spaceship. He'd use that as his target.

Xi Niu released the magic he kept inside of him. While he'd heard other magicians talk about calling their magic to them, drawing up their power, that wasn't what it felt like to him. For him, it was more like the magic was always there, churning inside of him like a dragon, held at bay by the thinnest of curtains. All he ever had to do was to pull that curtain to the side for the magic to come streaming out.

Xi Niu directed the first wave of magic just past the drone sitting outside of the spaceship. He had tried building portals that weren't as strong, but it never worked. The power rushed out of him, happy to have its head. He had to put on the brakes, shift it around, force it into a swirling oval.

Normally, the first thing a wizard did was to ground a

portal, generally by sprinkling ashes on the earth. Then they called up a series of characters into the air, each burning brightly with their own unique power. The characters had to be placed in an oval, floating in the air. Only after the characters were established could the wizard utter a transformation spell, transmuting the characters into a portal to another place.

Larger portals required more characters. The smallest ones needed fewer than half a dozen.

The characters that were used depended on both the wizard as well as where the portal was going. However, the center character was always the same, *men*, the Chinese character for "gate." It was the key character directing the location the portal would open up to.

A floating portal wasn't grounded, so no ash was necessary. The characters were only in a wizard's head and weren't conjured into the air, flaming in an oval. It was a much more complicated spell in some ways. If the characters were actually drawn with fire, the wizard only had to concentrate on keeping them floating.

If the characters were in the wizard's head, the magician had to pay attention to the configuration and keep the image strong as well as do everything else.

Many wizards could only do grounded portals. It wasn't that they didn't have the strength, but they had difficulty splitting their attention that way. Xi Niu had found that the floating portals he did with Kan Li and Ao Dan were easier in some ways than the grounded ones, primarily because he was merely focused on creating an opening, not on where it was going. The character *men* stayed floating in the center, unseen and unused.

It gratified him when the spinning gray portal opened up right where he'd placed it, just in front of them, close to the drone. The abyss in the center of it was much blacker than the night's sky. It had a different quality as well. If he were being fanciful, he'd say that it was soul sucking, while the darkness of space surrounding them, was just there and had no awareness.

He gave a thumbs-up to the others once it was complete. He couldn't really talk much while he was concentrating so hard.

Kan Li stepped up beside him and built her portal just a short distance away. They'd considered building the first portal all the way over on Mars, but they wanted to do just a small distance at first.

When Kan Li nodded to Xi Niu, he mentally flexed his knuckles. Now came the fun part.

He pulled the curtain back further on his magic, letting it flow all around him. Then he directed his energy outward, searching for the signature of Kan Li. They'd worked out a good system. She would be reaching for his portal at the same time he was reaching for hers.

At first, he'd failed when he'd tried linking to one of her portals that he couldn't see. They'd had to build a sensitivity to each other's magic. Though really, it was only when she'd started actively reaching for the portal that she could see in front of her that he'd been able to find hers.

Distance had also mattered. The farther away the portals, the longer it took to find and link them together. Fortunately, Xi Niu had power to spare.

He reached for Kan Li's portal. When he was about halfway there, it felt to him as though he met a second stream of power. This one, though, was red hot. Though Kan Li always smiled as she was a happy, lucky girl, Xi Niu assumed that she raged inside, all the time.

What made her so angry? He didn't know. He was pretty sure, though, that he didn't want to find out. He was equally certain that he never wanted all that anger directed at him.

Xi Niu followed Kan Li's stream back to the other portal, then started the hard work of linking the two portals together. Kan Li supported him as well as she could, keeping a beam of magic focused at his portal.

But she couldn't forge the links he could. He wasn't even sure how he was able to do it. The image always formed in his mind that he was building a chain between the two portals. The metal of each link was as big around as his thigh. They shone like brightly polished silver, but were as cold as the vacuum of space.

The first chain always took longer than the others. That was okay. Xi Niu knew he could do this.

The rest of the chains were easier, flowing out from his mind, connecting the two openings. Then he flattened out the chains, building them into solid sheets of steel, a tunnel flowing from one portal to the other.

He could always tell when he was finished and the portals were solidly linked. It wasn't an audible clicking noise, but it felt that way, like how two pieces of a puzzle would click together and make a whole.

It took more concentration once he had the portals connected. He didn't try to talk, but just nodded, holding his hands behind his back, like a soldier at rest. He couldn't physically see the link between the two portals—no one could—but he could sense that it was there.

Now, it was Ryan's turn. Xi Niu couldn't turn his head to watch, but he knew that the scientist was grinning.

The little lights of the drone moved away, centering on the middle of the portal Xi Niu had built. Ryan pushed one of the knobs forward, sliding the drone easily through the portal.

However, something was wrong. Xi Niu could tell immediately, though it took him a few moments for his eyes to catch up with what his magic felt.

The drone slid right out of the tunnel Xi Niu had built. It sat on the far side of the portal, blinking. It had never made it to Kan Li's portal. It had never disappeared into the portal.

Xi Niu risked a glance at Kan Li, only to find her staring at him.

"Try it again," she ordered Ryan, never taking her eyes of Xi Niu.

Xi Niu turned and looked out into space again. *Come on*, he silently urged the little drone.

He was certain that Ryan could sense the portal. Even if he wasn't strong enough to build one himself, he had to have enough magical sense to be able to see it.

However, the drone, it appeared, couldn't. It acted as if neither the tunnel nor the portal was there.

"The portals are connected. I swear they are," Xi Niu said through gritted teeth. He checked the links between the two portals. There wasn't a hole that he could find. The tunnel had clicked when it had been solidly formed.

What had he done wrong? They'd been able to shove blocks through their portals back on Earth.

Ryan tried flying the drone through a third time, with the same result.

"Kill the portal," Ao Dan directed.

Xi Niu pulled the curtain over his power, cutting off the flow to the portal, feeling both it and the tunnel collapse in on itself.

He turned to the older magicians, feeling as unsure as his years made him.

"We'll try it again," Ao Dan said.

Why was he glaring at Kan Li and not at Xi Niu?

"Though I doubt we'll have different results," Ao Dan added.

Kan Li glowered back at him. "Fine," she said. Then she turned on Xi Niu. "You're sure the portals were connected?"

"I am," Xi Niu said, as certain as he could be.

What was wrong? What had he done wrong?

When Xi Niu connected his portal to Ao Dan, he tried to build stronger links between the two portals. It wasn't possible for him to double up the links, though he did try to add extra ones.

Once again, the drone flew through the opening as if it weren't there.

Xi Niu didn't dare ask what was wrong, though he thought it really hard at all of the adults in the room. He didn't understand the underlying storm that appeared to be raging between Kan Li and Ao Dan.

Kan Li finally appeared to take pity on him. "Portals only work when there's consciousness involved," she told him quietly. "It's why the company can't just shove boxes from one warehouse to another. Machines and inanimate objects can't find the portal, can't react to it." She sighed.

"Now, we need to find us a pilot."

***

XI NIU FELT a small measure of relief that the others weren't blaming him for the failure of their test that day.

However, he still felt guilty about it, as if he were at fault somehow.

Xi Niu took a lot of deep breaths when they reached the Earth again, when he could finally breathe real air and not canned. His legs wobbled when gravity got ahold of them. He walked behind the others though the retractable tunnel that led from the spaceship to the port. Ao Dan and Kan Li seriously discussed the issue as they walked, ignoring him.

There wasn't anything Xi Niu could add to their conversation anyway. He didn't know enough.

Like his namesake, he was just the muscle, not the brains of this operation.

He still listened.

The problem was that while *Huli* Transport certainly had pilots on its payroll, none of them were wizards. They were all mundane. It had never come up before, that a space pilot might need magic.

How long were they going to have to wait to find a wizard willing to take flight training? How much training did they need before they'd be ready to go? They wouldn't be able to use the automated systems, that was certain. Did the ship itself have to have additional shielding?

Ao Dan described how cold Henry had grown when he'd come through a distant tunnel himself. They could send a messenger through if they were in a full EVA suit. Would they survive a really long journey, though? Who should they recruit?

Xi Niu couldn't help but glance out the window at the rainy landscape just beyond the spaceport. It had been built just a few miles away from the old San Francisco airport, south of the city. Empty space surrounded them, no houses or other buildings in sight, just trees in the distance, across a marshy wetland.

He couldn't wait to get outside and actually feel the rain on his skin. Still, he hesitated, wanting to add something to the conversation, though he didn't know what.

Being a messenger was a dangerous occupation. Xi Niu knew that. Between the monsters of the world suddenly able to sense you, as well as the occasional hitchhikers coming through a portal, messengers frequently didn't make it to their five-year anniversary with the company.

The company paid a lot in death benefits, which was why

they still found recruits. In addition, there was always the potential promise of becoming a wizard. Or at the very least, being absorbed somewhere into the corporate structure as a manager.

It wasn't employment for life. People could still get fired, particularly if they turned to chaotic magic or drugs, or if they were caught stealing from the company. However, most people who joined the company stayed. Where else could a wizard get full-time employment, plus benefits?

Xi Niu had heard his uncle once joke about how working for *Huli* Transport was similar in some ways to working for the Mafia—death was the way most people retired.

Still, sending a messenger just wearing an EVA suit sounded like a death sentence to him, even if the messenger had a propulsion pack on and so could push themselves through the tunnel.

When Ao Dan and Kan Li had a pause, Xi Niu blurted out, "Is there some way the messenger could be in a ship, or even a protected box, and then one of us could propel them through the tunnel? That way they'd be safer, more protected."

The two turned to look at him, as if they'd forgotten he was still there. "That's a possibility," Ao Dan said, nodding.

Kan Li appeared to be considering it. "We've never tried it before," she said slowly. "But it could work."

"Good," Xi Niu said.

While maybe he couldn't make a tunnel that would work with an automated system, maybe he could build one strong enough for a manned box to travel along.

It was worth a try.

<hr>

XI NIU SAT on his bed, shivering. All his sheets were

tangled up. He couldn't hear anyone moving beyond the closed door to his bedroom. No one else was up in the apartment that he'd grown up in with his parents and younger sister. The air still carried the scents from dinner, of fried ginger and fish.

The nightmare had followed him home, as he'd suspected it would.

The poor messenger screaming as the box slid out of the tunnel and into the abyss. The darkness there, consuming her soul.

And it had been Xi Niu's idea! The death of the messenger Gan Ji was on his head and no one else's. Sure, the messengers knew it was dangerous. And her family would be well taken care of.

They'd tried sending a messenger through with just a propulsion pack. While that had worked well on Earth, it had only worked for a short distance in space. The first time they'd tried it out there, the messenger hadn't been able to find the tunnel, and so slid through like the drone did.

The second messenger never made it to the distant portal.

They'd tried putting the messenger inside a box that Ao Dan could push along the tunnel. That had been Gan Ji.

At least no one had suggested that they try sending another messenger through that way.

No, it appeared that the messenger had to travel through on their own power, in a vehicle of some sort. Like a messenger on a motorcycle.

That meant building an even larger portal, one that could accommodate a spaceship.

It wouldn't take Xi Niu and his partners long to figure out how to do that.

The problem was still finding a pilot. It would take at least two weeks for the most basic crash course on flying a spaceship. Though much of flying a spaceship was automated, a lot of that automation couldn't be relied on, not in this situation.

Plus, the spaceship itself had to be stripped down, the engines and other system shielded from going through the tunnel.

Xi Niu groaned and dropped onto his back, staring up at the ceiling. "Time?" he said quietly. The clock flashed the numbers up where he could see them—2:15 A.M.

He sighed. He wasn't sure when he was going to get back to sleep. That nightmare…those screams…

Yeah. May as well get online and see if any of his friends were up and could chat with him. He might even tell them about his nightmare, though he knew they'd tease him.

All they knew was that he worked for a Chinese shipping company called *Huli* Transport, and that his uncle had gotten him the job. It was getting harder to talk with them, as Xi Niu had to hide so many secrets, now.

But he stubbornly continued to try. He couldn't leave his friends behind. Particularly not when he hadn't really made any new ones.

He grabbed a ratty sweatshirt and some sweatpants, sliding those on before he walked over to the computer humming to itself in the corner. He slid on the first sensory glove and considered the second, maybe going and smashing some bad guys in a game, but that felt like too much effort.

Besides, he couldn't stand to hear more screams just then.

Bian Shay's avatar—a great snake goddess, with the head of a beautiful woman and the torso and tail of a golden serpent—appeared in the lower corner of his screen when he flicked it on. Her status read "Fixing tea," so he knew that she'd be back soon. He waved at her, his own icon a dark magician with a navy-blue cloak and a tall, pointed hat.

Bian Shay waved back almost immediately. Her avatar slithered into an open room owned by their group. Xi Niu followed. The two figures appeared like holograms projected up from his desk, each about eight inches tall. The room sprang up around them, looking like an ancient library in a tower, round with bookshelves filling all the walls. Xi Niu had the scent turned off, but he could still smell the leather and musty paper in his head.

"You're up late," Bian Shay said, sipping her tea. A gorgeous red and gold silk robe covered the human part of her. Swords poked up over each shoulder. Her long black hair was held back with jeweled hair pins that doubled as deadly darts in the game.

Xi Niu wished that he had something similar for his avatar to do instead of standing there stupidly. "Couldn't sleep," he said. It was close enough to the truth.

"Nightmares?" Bian Shay guessed.

The shiver that Xi Niu gave translated to his avatar and was more than enough response.

"It's working for that company, isn't it?" Bian Shay said, the glare from her avatar strong enough for Xi Niu to feel the heat.

He didn't know what Bian Shay had against *Huli* Transport. Of all his friends, she'd been the only one to express concern over his new position. Everyone else had just insisted that he buy the next round of drinks, though he drew the line at taking them all out to dinner.

"Kind of," Xi Niu said. There wasn't a lot he could say, despite how he might want to.

Bian Shay stepped to the side, so that instead of facing his avatar, they stood shoulder to shoulder. "You know," she said in the softest possible voice, "there are other companies."

"Other transportation companies?" Xi Niu asked, not sure exactly what his friend was saying.

Bian Shay nodded solemnly. "Other companies that

deliver the same sorts of messages. To the same sorts of beings."

"I'm not sure what you're talking about," Xi Niu said. Did *Huli* Transport have rivals? He'd never heard about their competition. He didn't recall his uncle ever mentioning them.

Of course, there must be others trying to do the same business. Not just in the mundane world, but when dealing with the gods, right?

What other companies were there? Did they have wizards on staff as well?

Bian Shay gave Xi Niu an exasperated sigh. "Are you really that dense?"

"No," Xi Niu said. "Just cautious."

Bian Shay blinked, her avatar's face going blank for a moment. "Oh. Okay," she said.

"You want to go have tea tomorrow night?" Xi Niu asked. He didn't want to talk about anything regarding the company or magic on a public forum. While he and his friends paid for the private room they chatted in, as well as for some level of privacy, his generation had learned early on that meat-space was the only private space available anymore. And even then, you could be recorded at any time.

However, anything said online, even on homegrown servers, was frequently still recorded and could be subpoenaed by a court.

"Meet me at Quantum Cats. At eight tomorrow night," Bian Shay directed Xi Niu before her avatar swept out of the room.

"Okay," Xi Niu said, his avatar standing alone in the meeting room.

He sat back in his chair, tilting his head toward the ceiling again. Though he was tired, he couldn't go back to sleep. Not yet.

Might as well go and kill some imaginary monsters. He slid on the second sensory glove and made a fist. A flaming sword appeared in the hands of his avatar, and the library melted away into a forest.

Showtime.

XI NIU WAITED at a table in the back for Bian Shay to show up. She was late, which wasn't like her. He sipped a lovely ginger and hibiscus tea. The café was surprisingly crowded, not only students hogging the tables with their screens and readers, but tourists as well. Xi Niu had managed to snag one of the last tables.

Soft pop music played in the background, by a band he didn't recognize. Then again, popular bands rarely lasted more than a couple weeks anymore before the next new best thing happened. Conversations around him weren't really distinguishable, probably due to some inaudible white noise run through the air. The smell of the scones and other pastries was really strong, probably piped in with the music. He'd had a big dinner, though, so wasn't hungry. At least for now.

He amused himself by watching the cats.

The Quantum Cat café had between five to seven real cats strolling around between the tables, looking for someone to pet them as well as for scraps. There were also just as many hologram cats doing the same thing.

The far wall of the café wasn't real, but a hologram as well. To Xi Niu it looked like a fuzzy curtain, though he knew that to everyone else, it appeared as a solid white wall, with 3-D artwork hanging on it, some sort of still life with neo-colored fruit and cats.

Cats wandered through the wall on a regular basis,

seeming to just disappear. As there was a large cat tree on the other side of the hologram wall, the cats would sometimes appear to be jumping out of midair back into the café.

It was a clever concept, and had been pretty successful. They were actually a chain, and frequently swapped cats between the cafés so that customers had to keep guessing which cats were real and which weren't.

Xi Niu never had to guess. The hologram cats all had an extra glow to them.

Finally, Bian Shay came hurrying in. She glanced around the café, spotting him and waving before she went to order her tea from the hologram standing behind the automated machine at the counter.

Xi Niu studied his friend carefully. Did she have magic? Once he'd learned that he did, back when he was fifteen, he'd checked them all to see if maybe one of them did.

As they hadn't at that time, he'd never bothered rechecking any of them.

There. One of the tiny rings that pierced her upper earlobe had magic. It wasn't very strong, but it glowed steadily. It must be a type of battery for her.

Huh. He didn't wonder why she'd never said anything. You weren't supposed to say anything to mundanes. Ever.

He wished he'd known earlier. However, how cool was it that he was finally going to have someone to talk with!

"Breakdown," Bian Shay said with an exaggerated sigh when she came over and put her teacup down.

He nodded. Though the superfast trains that had replaced the existing BART system were generally much better than the older ones, much more reliable and always clean, they still broke down now and again.

Xi Niu waited until Bian Shay had shrugged off her red and gold raincoat, revealing an emerald colored green shirt, before he leaned across the table and said quietly, "You didn't tell me."

Bian Shay shrugged. "You didn't tell me either," she said.

"So when did you find out? Are you studying to be a wizard? Tell me everything!" Xi Niu said. He couldn't contain his excitement. Maybe he could recruit her for *Huli* Transport. He thought he'd read on one of the bulletin boards about some sort of bonus you'd get for bringing a new employee into the company.

Bian Shay gave an exaggerated sigh. "Keep your voice down," she said. "No, I'm not a wizard. Not everyone has the power of an ox."

Xi Niu grinned at her. He couldn't help what he had. He wasn't surprised that she knew, though.

"I work for a…different transportation company," she said. "Much smaller than *Huli* Transport. Yamamoto Logistics."

"They're a Japanese company, right?" Xi Niu said, trying to recall what Bian Shay had told him when she'd first gotten a job there in the back office, over a year before, while he'd still been in school.

"They are," Bian Shay said. "But they have many of the same clientele as *Huli* Transport. The same contacts both here and…elsewhere."

Xi Niu wasn't sure why she was so hesitant about mentioning the gods, immortals, and heroes that he knew *Huli* Transport supplied.

"Why didn't you say anything when I told you I was going to work for *Huli* Transport?" Xi Niu said.

"I did try to warn you against going to work for them," Bian Shay said. "And I'm right, aren't I? You regret your choice."

Xi Niu shrugged. He wasn't sure he regretted his choice.

It was just…they had a problem to solve and it was costing them lives.

When Bian Shay continued to stare at him, Xi Niu finally responded. "I'm not sure regret is the right word. There are just some things going on that are hard right now."

"*Huli* Transport has no concern for human life," Bian Shay stated bluntly. "They run through their messengers like they're a dime a dozen, killing off at least half of them in the process. They pay huge death benefits, as well as enormous bribes to keep officials from noticing just how many people die in service to the company."

Xi Niu bit his lips together. While he didn't think the company was that bad, he knew that there was an element of truth in Bian Shay's words. Just a couple weeks ago he'd listened to a group of wizards casually brush off the death of a messenger as if it were just a piece of paper that had gone missing. Neither Ao Dan or Kan Li seemed very affected by the deaths that they'd caused, from sending messengers through tunnels in space.

Only Xi Niu appeared to be bothered by all of that.

"And you're saying that Yamamoto Logistics is different? That they don't kill off as many messengers?" Xi Niu asked.

"That's right," Bian Shay said with pride. "They're a much more humane company. When we lose a messenger, everyone knows. There are little black icons on all the message boards. Tell me, does *Huli* even keep track of the number they've lost?"

Xi Niu couldn't answer that. "I'm sure they keep track," he said after a few moments.

"What kind of safeguards do they have in place to keep the messengers intact?" Bian Shay said, pressing her point. "Do they turn down the dangerous contracts? Or do they take them and just charge more, knowing that they'll pay out more death benefits as a result?"

"I don't know," Xi Niu said. "I'm not in that part of the business." He wasn't. He wasn't responsible for contracts and those sorts of things.

Just the death of at least a couple of messengers, like Gan Ji the day before.

"Come into my office tomorrow night, after work," Bian Shay said. "Meet with my manager. There's a different way of operating. You don't have to stay with *Huli* Transport."

Xi Niu wasn't sure what to say. He actually kind of thought he did have to stay. He'd signed a non-compete clause in his contract, along with lots of other papers. He hadn't read them that carefully, and wasn't sure what all of them said, though he believed that he'd have to work there for at least a few years, or else pay them money for the wizard training they were giving him.

Plus, he'd signed a bunch more papers just the last few weeks swearing him to secrecy when it came to the beacons and such.

"*Huli* Transport doesn't own your soul," Bian Shay said. "Or at least, not yet."

Xi Niu shivered. Maybe it would be good to keep his options open, to see what Yamamoto Logistics could offer him.

He was pretty sure they wouldn't be able to offer him the stars. Not like *Huli* Transport.

Still. It wouldn't hurt to go talk with Bian Shay's manager. Right?

THE MAIN HEADQUARTERS for *Huli* Transport were in downtown San Francisco. It didn't take that long by train to get there from Walnut Creek, where Xi Niu had grown up. However, Yamamoto Logistics was located south of the metropolitan area, near the old airport. It wasn't that far of a ride from downtown, but he was in for a really long trek on his way back home.

Fortunately, Xi Niu had left himself a lot of time, slurping down noodles in the train station then getting on board, as he didn't want to be late and make a bad impression.

Instead of being at the top of a thirty-story tower, the company's offices were on the second and third floors of a set of connected buildings that sprawled across an entire city block. The first floor was all taken up with loading docks for trucks.

Xi Niu assumed that Yamamoto also had a mundane shipping arm. Maybe they had started out that way, even.

A set of glass doors was wedged in between two of the loading areas at one end of the building. It surprised Xi Niu that they were protected with magic, as the golden-brass metal holding the glass in place had a special glow to it.

Why would the front doors need to be covered in magic? Were they expecting some sort of attack? Or was this just one of the extra sorts of protection that Bian Shay claimed the company regularly employed?

Xi Niu felt a strong current when he touched the door handle. Not to shock him, no, but to taste him, to see if he was friend or foe. Possibly also to measure his magic.

A receptionist smiled at him from behind her desk, just to the right of the doors. A large YLI logo projected in 3-D floated above her head. The colors were a loud blue and silver, more like a sports team colors than a company's colors.

"Wang Xi Niu, yes?" she asked. "I've already notified Mr. Sato that you've arrived. Please take a seat."

Xi Niu almost protested that there was some mistake. He could have sworn that Bian Shay's manager was a woman.

Maybe he was wrong. Or maybe instead of meeting with

Bian Shay's manager, he was going to meet with a recruiter instead.

Xi Niu looked at the small lobby to his right. Three form-fitting chairs had been lined up against the windows looking out on the trucks and the parking lot. Even from where he stood he could tell they were older models, lumpy, the gel inside them probably needing to be replaced. The other chairs were plain upholstery, the kind his grandmother had in her living room. They looked equally as shabby and uncomfortable.

Before Xi Niu could move into the lobby, a man came through the door just to the left of the reception area. He wasn't much taller than Xi Niu, maybe five foot eight, and was built on the same slight lines as Xi Niu.

But that was where the similarities ended. Xi Niu would bet that he was Japanese-American, based on his eyes and his darker skin color, as well as his big nose. His black hair was peppered with white, giving him a distinguished look. The black suit he wore probably cost as much as what Xi Niu made in a month. His white shirt had a high collar, done in a light blue. The button that closed it had a shining red jewel in the center of it that glowed at Xi Niu.

Magic.

"Ah, so good to meet you, Mr. Wang," Mr. Sato said, bowing and not attempting to shake Xi Niu's hand.

It was so weird to be called Mr. Wang! That was his dad's name. But Xi Niu understood the need for the formality. He wasn't about to give this foreign wizard permission to use his personal name.

"I've heard all about you from your friend, Ms. Chan," Mr. Sato said, turning and leading Xi Niu back through the door. A long narrow hallway appeared to run the length of the building. It smelled of the ozone and corn gas that was used to power the trucks. Just a few steps beyond the door stood a staircase going up to the next level.

"Are you her manager?" Xi Niu asked.

"No, no, that isn't my position," Mr. Sato said with a smile. "Please, won't you join me here?" Mr. Sato said, leading Xi Niu to a conference room right behind the staircase.

Walking through the doorway felt like walking through an electric curtain. Only when Xi Niu was on the other side did he realize that it was a magical barrier. He glanced at the walls. They had that same blue paint on them that the walls of the spaceship had, meant to contain any magical energy.

Huh. The only rooms like that in *Huli* HQ were the portal rooms, so that any hitchhikers who came through unexpected on a portal couldn't get out into the rest of the building. Even the labs where he'd been working with Ao Dan and Kan Li hadn't been shielded this way.

No stray magic was getting in or out of this room. No one was going to scry on them in here.

Maybe there was something to Bian Shay's claims that *Huli* didn't take care of its people very well.

A small conference table took up most of the center of the room, with half a dozen metal and leather chairs arranged around it. No windows on the walls. No pictures either. The industrial brown carpet muted sounds well, though. The air in here smelled stale, canned but without good filters.

Xi Niu turned down the offer of water, coffee, or tea. He really just wanted to hear what Mr. Sato had to say.

Mr. Sato pressed a button on the edge of the table. A hologram sprang up in the center of it. A Japanese girl in her twenties, about ten inches tall, stood there, wearing a red-and-white striped shirt with a black vest and pants. Cat ears stuck up out of her long black hair. They looked soft and white, tufted at the tops, like a lynx. Her nose appeared to be black, and long gray whiskers flowed down from either side. She bowed gravely to Xi Niu.

Who was she? Was this an avatar? What sort of corporate leader would choose to be represented by such a figure?

"See-tza Young Yamamoto, our founder, started Yamamoto Logistics over one hundred and fifty years ago," Mr. Sato announced proudly.

Xi Niu blinked, surprised. Wait. Those ears were real? Not an avatar? What, did that mean that the company had been formed by a being who wasn't human?

"She saw a niche that wasn't being filled by *Huli* Transport and ruthlessly moved to exploit it," Mr. Sato continued.

Xi Niu felt his eyebrows raise. This wasn't the usual recruitment speech that the manager generally gave, he was certain of it.

"*Huli* Transport focuses primarily on the gods, immortals, and heroes," Mr. Sato said. See-tza Yamamoto was replaced with a series of figures who Xi Niu recognized from his own training with *Huli* Transport, Zhong Gua Lao, Hou Fi Don, and others.

"However, there are many races besides the humans who exist both on this world and in between," Mr. Sato explained. A figure Xi Niu had never seen before appeared, almost human though with a long, pale white fish face. Then a tree-like figure appeared, followed by an ugly face that appeared to be encrusted with dirt and unpolished stones.

"*Huli* Transport has ignored the other races for far too long, assuming that the profit margin was too small to be worth their time or effort," Mr. Sato said, the condemnation obvious in his voice. "However, as Yamamoto Logistics has taken care of the little people, the races left to manage on their own, not only has their business grown, but their reputation as well."

Now an image appeared, showing Zhong Gua Lao bowing low to Mr. Sato.

Huh. Only the really important people at *Huli* Transport met with the immortals and other beings. Mr. Sato must be fairly high in the company. Why was he talking with Xi Nui?

"We have been able to strike deals with many of the individuals who solely used *Huli* Transport in the past," Mr. Sato said proudly. "We are gaining market share, but more importantly, mind share. Immortals and gods are now seeking us out for their business."

Xi Niu knew nothing of that. But it made sense to him that if *Huli* Transport really wasn't serving all clients, then someone else would come along and do the job instead.

"Our messengers are accorded every conceivable protection," Mr. Sato continued.

A figure of a *Huli* Transport messenger popped up. He was wearing the typical company leathers, carrying a motorcycle helmet in one hand.

The leathers expanded outward, showing an exploded view of all the layers of protection that were included in the leathers.

There weren't many. Even Xi Niu could see that. The material was all reinforced with steel threads, so that a crash at high speeds wouldn't necessarily kill the wearer. The helmet, too, was specially reinforced.

But that was about it.

Then the color of the leather changed from the brown and red of the *Huli* company colors to a much cooler red and blue. Layers of additional protection were added, like next to the messenger's skin, as well as more built in around the joints and across the shoulders. The helmet had a different type of hardened steel added to it, that Mr. Sato assured Xi Niu was both stronger as well as lighter.

Overall, the messenger was just more protected.

Why didn't *Huli* do that sort of thing?

Next, Mr. Sato showed the portal rooms that Yamamoto used. They also had more protection built into them. He showed a simulation of a wizard casting a portal. It surprised Xi Niu that the first thing the wizard did was to call a detection spell. Wouldn't everything in the room show up as magical already?

But no, it had a specific focus to it—to detect how close the portal was to any sort of hitchhiker. By using this detection spell, the wizard would be able to collapse the portal before a messenger went through if he or she got a positive hit.

Huh. That seemed so obvious. Again, why didn't *Huli* Transport do that sort of thing? Particularly when it appeared to be such a simple spell? It didn't even appear to need any additional ingredients.

At the end of the presentation, Mr. Sato gave Xi Niu a huge, salesman's smile. "So you see, there are several differences between the two companies. Which one, though, is the smarter choice?"

"You've given me a lot to think about," Xi Niu said. He wasn't about to make such an important decision right there. "I will need to carefully consider what you say."

"Are you sure?" Mr. Sato asked. "The choice seems obvious. Come. Let me show you the rest of our operation. That will help you decide."

Xi Niu shook his head. "No, thank you," he said firmly. "You've given me enough to think about."

Mr. Sato pressed. "It will only take a few minutes. You will be very impressed, I think."

"No," Xi Niu said softly as he stood up. "I would like to go home and think on what you've shown me."

He could tell that Mr. Sato wanted to push more. But it would have been impossible for him to compel Xi Niu to do anything he didn't want to. He could be as stubborn as an ox when he needed to be. In addition, he was wary, now. And strong. No magic could compel him.

He really needed to talk with someone from *Huli* Transport. There had to be a reason why they didn't protect their messengers better. It wasn't just because they had a general disregard for human life, was it? There had to be something else.

"I think you're making a mistake," Mr. Sato said slowly as he stood. "You need to decide which side you're on. Now."

"Why are you pushing this?" Xi Niu asked, confused. He didn't understand why he needed to make a decision immediately. This wasn't something he was about to jump into with both feet, not without looking around really carefully first.

Mr. Sato gave a bitter sounding laugh. "I'll never have the opportunity to talk with you again. You will be warned away from us."

"They can't stop me," Xi Niu said, confused.

"You are so young," Mr. Sato said. "So naïve. You have no idea the sort of company you work for. Ah well. Don't say that you weren't warned."

He gave Xi Niu a deep bow. "It was very nice meeting you. I hope you survive the next few weeks."

"It was nice meeting you as well," Xi Niu said, returning the bow then leaving the room.

It was probably just his imagination that the curtain of power separating the room from the hallway was thicker this time, as if it wanted to impede him from going through.

Xi Niu didn't let it even slow him down as he stalked out of the Yamamoto Logistics headquarters and back to the train station.

He needed to talk with someone at *Huli* headquarters about what had just happened.

But who?

———

IT DIDN'T SURPRISE Xi Niu in the least when Ao Dan came and sat next to him on the train going back to Walnut Creek, just two stations after he'd boarded the train. The older wizard wore a subdued (for him) purple sequined jacket and searing bright red pants tucked into black boots with a disturbing white design on them that kept moving and twisting, like snakes dancing.

"So you went to Yamamoto Logistics," Ao Dan said.

Xi Niu pressed his lips together and stared forward, into the train itself. The walls and seats were made from a blue-green plastic that healed itself. If some tagger or other graffiti artist tried marking it, the mark would be consumed by the plastic within a few hours. It made the seats cold and hard, but the trains were now always clean.

As Ao Dan didn't say anything else, Xi Niu finally replied, "So what if I did?"

Ao Dan sighed and shook his head. "You are so young. So naïve."

Xi Niu bristled. Mr. Sato had said the exact same thing. Though Ao Dan sounded sadder when he said it than Mr. Sato had.

"I blurred your path and image," Ao Dan said softly. "No one else will know that you made the trip."

That surprised Xi Niu. "Really? Was that necessary?"

Ao Dan gave a mirthless laugh. "It was," he said, his tone harsh and grim. "What did you tell them?"

"What do you mean?" Xi Niu asked, surprised.

"What did you tell them of the beacons?" Ao Dan said.

"Nothing!" Xi Niu said. Then he put it together. "Oh. You think I'm a spy! That I was carrying corporate secrets to the competition. I wasn't. Honest. I didn't tell them anything about the beacons. They were just trying to recruit me, as a wizard. I have a friend who works there."

Ao Dan stared at him for a moment, before he nodded. "Smart of them, really. They didn't want to get you killed by bringing up the real reason why they had you come in. But do you really think that they just wanted to hire you away?"

"Yes?" Xi Niu said, uncertain.

Ao Dan snorted with derision. "You're an untrained wizard. Just as likely to blow yourself up as anyone else. You don't have the control you need. Power is easy to come by. Control, discipline, isn't. Do you really think they want an inexperienced boy just because he's strong?"

"I don't know," Xi Niu said. He'd assumed they'd just wanted him, for, well, himself. How was he to know it was all a ruse?

However, it made more sense now, how Mr. Sato had pushed, trying to recruit him. As well as why Mr. Sato was in upper management, and not lower down.

Xi Nui sat and thought for a moment. The train pulled up into the next station silently, then took off again at high speed. More people got on and off, going about their regular business.

"You said you hid me, right? So that no one is going to know where I went tonight?" Xi Niu asked after a moment.

"I did," Ao Dan said, nodding.

"What would have happened if you hadn't done that? Or if someone at *Huli* HQ does find out?" Xi Niu said.

Ao Dan shrugged. "Beyond an official reprimand? Not sure. Probably threats to your family and loved ones."

"What?" Xi Niu said.

Ao Dan glared at him for shouting, but he couldn't help himself.

"Are you serious?" Xi Niu said after a moment. "They'd start threatening my family?"

Ao Dan appeared to be choosing his words carefully. "You have an uncle in the company, yes?"

"I do," Xi Niu said. He'd never been close to his uncle, his father's older brother, Jing Po.

"Go ask him," Ao Dan said, rising. "And if you do decide to go back to Yamamoto Logistics, hide your own damned trail next time."

"I will," Xi Niu promised, though he still felt bewildered by the need.

"And I'd consider changing your friends as well," Ao Dan warned as he sashayed off.

Xi Niu couldn't help but roll his eyes at the aging queen, who seemed determined to outshine all the rest of the mere mortals on the train.

Was he right, though? Did Xi Niu have a reason to be worried?

He sent a message to his uncle, then spent the rest of the long ride home staring out the window at the wet landscape, lit by neon and holograms, wondering about the road he'd chosen, and whether he needed to hold onto it or not.

JING PO INVITED Xi Niu to his apartment in west San Francisco, the Haight Ashbury area. He lived in one of the newer condos out there, a building that had been more grown than built, with huge vats of chemicals poured into forms. It made the building much more resilient. While the sonic dampeners would take the sting out of any earthquake that shook the area, the newer buildings could withstand a much larger shock as they'd roll with the earth, bending and not breaking.

Xi Niu didn't remember that Jing Po had at least half of the top floor of his building until he got out there. Windows stretched from floor to ceiling on three sides of the open living room and kitchen area. He could have fit two, maybe three, of the condos he and his parents shared into just this space alone.

The floors were a dark mahogany, and would have been incredibly expensive if they were made from real wood. Artwork was projected in front of the windows, easy to take down or move around so as not to spoil the view. Uncomfortable looking sofas and chairs were scattered across the floor. The only comfy spot was in the far left corner, a wingback reading chair made from a dark green upholstery, with a light standing next to it as well as a small stool for resting your feet on.

To the right was a solid wall with a closed door—Jing Po's bedroom. A large kitchen took up most of the rest of that wall, with a bathroom tucked away behind it. Like the rest of the space, the kitchen looked modern and high end as well as never used.

Now that Xi Niu was thinking about it, he realized that his uncle looked like an older edition of his father. Which made sense, as Jing Po was probably ten years older than his dad. They both had the same broad forehead and deep-set eyes. Jing Po weighed less than his dad, and his flat cheeks verged on gaunt. They both had thin lips and a small nose, with a soft chin rounding out the face.

Xi Niu resembled his mother much more, as his features were finer and slighter.

"Come in! Come in," Jing Po said, the cheer in his tone sounding forced. Jing Po had never married, but he'd been there for most of the family celebrations that Xi Niu remembered growing up. He wore a white business shirt and gray dress slacks, though instead of shoes he did wear a comfortable looking pair of black slipper socks.

Xi Niu took off his shoes just inside the door, along with his rain jacket. House slippers were in a basket just beside the door. Though he doubted that Jing Po's expensive floors could be marred by either dirt or water, it was still custom to remove one's shoes upon entering a home.

"I was just making some tea," Jing Po said. It surprised Xi Niu that his uncle was doing it the old-fashioned way, with a kettle on the stove. No one made tea that way anymore. There were self-heating cups that would warm the water to the perfect temperature. There were even instant cups that had the tea infused into the sides of the cup, so all you had to do was add water and stir.

"Sit," Jing Po directed as he went back into the kitchen.

Xi Niu sat down on one of the stools that were on the far side of the breakfast bar. It automatically adjusted itself so that he was at the perfect height, the footstool also rising up for him to put his toes on it. The padded gel conformed to him instantly, making him comfortable. Oh, nice! It also warmed up.

Nothing better than a butt warmer.

A comfortable silence filled the space as Jing Po actually boiled water in a kettle. Xi Niu knew that Jing Po wasn't that old, and certainly not as old as Ao Dan. But maybe he took comfort in rituals that had been around since forever.

The smell of a good ginger tea filled the area as Jing Po poured the water into a white porcelain teapot. It emitted a sharp blue light, which then faded down to nothing.

"The pot will start glowing brightly when the tea is finished," Jing Po told Xi Niu.

"Cool," Xi Niu said. He wasn't certain what he'd been expecting.

"So tell me what brings my oh-so-famous nephew out to see his old uncle," Jing Po said.

"Famous?" Xi Niu asked, confused. How could he be famous?

"You've been selected to work on some really important projects," Jing Po said proudly. "Now, I know you can't tell me about them. But word's gotten around about how you're such a rising star."

Xi Niu shook his head. "Thanks," he said. "It's an honor, really." He actually did feel that way about it sometimes.

"So what did you want to ask me about?" Jing Po said. "Outside of the office and away from anyone's scrying ears or eyes?"

It hadn't occurred to Xi Niu that anyone might try to listen in on their conversation. He really was going to have to start getting more paranoid, wasn't he?

"No one can hear us?" Xi Niu asked, making sure.

A brief glow of magic surged up the windows, outlined each one, before it died back down. "Nobody is getting through that," Jing Po said.

"Thank you," Xi Niu said. He sighed, considering the best way to proceed. "I have a friend. One of my best friends. Bian Shay. She works for Yamamoto Logistics, and—"

"Drop her," Jing Po said, interrupting.

"But—"

"You can no longer be friends with her," Jing Po said. "Don't meet with her privately. Ever. Don't take her comm calls. Don't hang out with her. You will need to turn your back on her."

"I don't understand," Xi Niu said, feeling much younger than his nineteen years.

"The company is very protective of its young wizards," Jing Po said. "Like a jealous lover. Don't ever, *ever*, give them the opportunity to question your loyalty."

"But that's not fair!" Xi Niu said. "Why can't I at least keep her as a friend?"

The teapot started to glow a bright blue, indicating that the tea was ready. Jing Po pulled out the basket with the loose leaf tea and set it aside before pouring the tea into two cups.

Xi Niu took a sip of the admittedly fine tea, the green tea component balancing nicely with the ginger, and sighed. He still didn't get it. It seemed like a stupid artificial rift between the two companies. Why couldn't everyone just get along?

"You are a very strong wizard, with a lot of power," Jing Po said slowly. "No one is ever going to be able to compel you to do something against your will. Not unless it's one of the gods."

Xi Niu couldn't help his shiver at that. He still didn't know why he'd said something about his headaches to Kan Li. Had it been one of the gods pushing him in the right direction?

"Not everyone is so strong," Jing Po continued. "They could be magically tHenryed into give away company secrets and not even realize they were doing it."

"Huh," Xi Niu said. He hadn't thought of that. But Bian Shay would never do that to him. Not that she could. She wasn't that strong of a magician.

Would Mr. Sato have tried to force Xi Niu to agree to stay there? If he'd thought he had a chance against Xi Niu's magic?

That he didn't know.

"So it's better to not have contact, just so that there's never any question," Jing Po said.

Though his uncle sounded quite reasonable, Xi Niu wasn't convinced.

"I'll think about it," Xi Niu said. It was the best answer he could give.

"What has your friend been telling you?" Jing Po asked.

Xi Niu took a sip of his tea, putting his words together before he replied. "She said that *Huli* Transport doesn't actually care for its messengers. That it doesn't provide the same amount of protection for them. Like extra layers of steel for their leathers, or extra detection spells that could be used when creating a portal. To make sure no hitchhikers were present."

It was totally reasonable that Bian Shay would ask about those things, right?

Jing Po narrowed his eyes at Xi Niu. "As for the messengers, they rejected wearing more steel. Said that it interferes with their magic. Shortens the timespan of a portal. They voted and unanimously turned it down."

"That's good to know," Xi Niu said. He *knew* that the company actually took better care of their messengers than they appeared to!

"A detection spell for a portal, though," Jing Po said, sounding thoughtful. "I hadn't heard about that. Tell me more."

Xi Niu tried to describe the spell as he'd seen it, how it was done without ingredients after the portal was formed. It was used to detect hitchhikers who were close or even in the portal tunnel.

"And Yamamoto Logistics wizards supposedly use such a spell every time they create a portal? Before they transport a messenger through?" Jing Po said.

"I've been told that, yes," Xi Niu said. Maybe both Mr. Sato and Bian Shay did know something that the company didn't.

"I'll look into it," Jing Po said. "Just know that it will take me some time, as I'm going to have to move slowly, cautiously, and not raise any suspicions."

"But you've already proven that you're loyal," Xi Niu said. "Why would you still have to be so cautious?"

"Because you have friends in other companies," Jing Po said with a tight smile. "And I'm much more expendable than you are."

"What does that mean?" Xi Niu asked. A sliver of fear had lodged itself firmly in the center of his belly.

"Working for *Huli* Transport is sort of like working for the Mafia," Jing Po said.

Xi Niu nodded. His uncle had said similar things in the past.

"Wizards never retire, you know," Jing Po continued. "They're generally killed while on the job. Frequently by one of those hitchhikers."

"Okay," Xi Niu said slowly. He still wasn't sure what Jing Po was hinting at.

His uncle took a sip of his tea and looked away, out the windows, into the darkness and the carpet of bright lights below. "No one has ever been able to prove whether or not *Huli* Transport has a way of calling hitchhikers to a portal or not. Of forcing wizards to retire that way."

Xi Niu blanched. That was horrible! And such an awful way to go, fighting a demon or some other horrible monster.

Jing Po turned and stared directly at Xi Niu, his dark eyes penetrating Xi Niu's soul, the words branding themselves there.

"If, *if* upper management at *Huli* HQ has such a spell, believe me, upper management at Yamamoto Logistics would have it as well," Jing Po said, his words ringing with a finality that made Xi Niu shiver again.

"Tell me how your father is doing," Jing Po said in a much lighter tone. "And your dear mother."

Xi Niu took the hint and just talked of trivial things until he finished his tea, before he took his leave. On the train home, he sat and considered everything his uncle had told him.

Had Xi Niu signed up for the Mafia by hiring on with *Huli* Transport? Why hadn't his uncle warned him away? Then again, how many other places would have work for a wizard? Particularly good paying work with benefits? Sure, there was universal healthcare, but having private or company-sponsored care was so much better.

At least now he understood how the company could threaten his family. He could see it now, his manager saying something like, "Got a really nice uncle there. Would be a shame for anything to happen to him."

But working for Yamamoto Logistics wouldn't be any better. He remembered their shabby offices and far-from-prime location.

And he believed his uncle that if *Huli* Transport could threaten his family, so could Yamamoto Logistics.

Xi Niu wasn't sure what he was going to do next. Turn Bian Shay away? Never see her again? But she was his friend! They'd gone through their last three years of school together, meeting twice a week to game with the group. She wasn't the only female in the half dozen of them, no, there was also Ti Li.

He was never going to meet with Mr. Sato again, that was certain.

The dark landscape outside the train windows held no clues to his future.

KAN LI and Ao Dan found half a dozen wizards who agreed to take a crash course in learning to fly spaceships. They'd all been able to detect the tunnels built between portals. The company was throwing a lot of resources at building new spaceships as well, that had a lot of additional shielding.

What would happen if it turned out that messengers

were no longer as important, and that pilots had to be wizards instead? Would the company disregard the messengers even more?

In the meantime, while wizards learned to be pilots, Xi Niu had a week "off." Instead of working with Ao Dan and Kan Li, Xi Niu had to go back to regular wizard training.

The training room wasn't located on the human plane. Instead, it was a private magical space that the teacher had carved out for them to practice in. Eight wizards were there that day to practice transformations.

Almost all magic was based on transformations. It was a skill that wizards kept improving on, no matter how many years of practice they already had. It was like martial arts in that way—as soon as you reached the equivalent of a black belt in a particular type of transformation, you went back to the beginning and started again, learning and applying more nuance and skill.

Portals were less about transformation and more about punching a hole through a space. Xi Niu had heard the theory that it actually *was* a transformation in one way—transforming positive space filled with something into negative space. That didn't feel right to him, though. Then again, he didn't have that much experience, despite the fact that he'd been creating a lot of different types of portals for the last few weeks.

The magical practice room looked like a gym, with soft gray pads on the floor and plain gray walls. Filtered light highlighted the entire ceiling, giving the room a comfortable glow. The air smelled fresher than Xi Niu expected—he figured that was part of the magic. The temperature was neither too hot nor too cold, though he'd heard about times when the teacher changed the room temperature frequently as a way to train wizards to not be distracted.

Today, the teacher, an older, white woman named

Gretchen, was leading them in an exercise that involved taking a small glass full of pebbles, transforming them into a solid wall, then turning around and dissolving the wall back into its original components, without destroying the pebbles in the process.

Xi Niu sat cross-legged on the floor in the back row. Two ragged lines of wizards sat in front of him. Most of the other students were young, just starting out, like him. However, an older gentleman in the first row had joined them, claiming that he needed the practice.

Continuing education was part of every wizard's life. Xi Niu had suspected that the man up front had just taken the class for the easy A.

Xi Niu poured the pebbles out of their glass container onto the floor in front of him. He picked up a few of them, feeling their rough surface between his fingers. He sniffed at them, not smelling the dirt he'd expected. Then again, they had been washed. The pebbles themselves were different shapes and sizes, from a round pea to half the length of his pinky finger. The color ranged from dark gray to light tan.

When Xi Niu looked up, he realized that most of the other students had already started. The older gentleman in the front row had built a red-brick wall with white mortar between the brick that he was carefully aging to make the wall look as though it had stood for ages. A couple of others had built concrete walls, while one had grown each pebble so the wall before her looked like a fieldstone wall.

Xi Niu concentrated on the small pile of stones in front of him. Gretchen had instructed them to build a wall that was familiar and not try to create a wall completely from their imaginations. Maybe try to build a wall from their apartment, or something that they passed by daily.

What sort of a wall did Xi Niu want to build?

He clutched at the first image that came to mind. He

mashed the pebbles together while trying to maintain their original form, so he wouldn't destroy them. Then he pushed the block up and out, spreading it like a baker would spread frosting up the side of tall cake. After that, he pushed outward, forming a wall as requested.

Color came next. He couldn't completely recreate the wild riot of flowers and vines that Ao Dan had spread across the hallway leading to their practice room. It still warmed his heart when he managed to at least get some of the brilliant reds and greens right.

"Interesting," Gretchen said.

Xi Niu looked up. He'd been so involved with building his wall that he hadn't noticed her approaching.

"Do the colors reach all the way through?" Gretchen asked. "Or are they just on the surface?"

Xi Niu had to look, because he wasn't sure. "All the way through," he said when he peered down at the wall. They'd saturated the plaster, making the middle just as colorful as either side.

"I see," Gretchen said. She obviously wasn't sure what to make of what he'd created.

Xi Niu felt his stubbornness rise up. He wasn't about to change his design. This was what had felt right to him.

When he looked around the room, he realized that his wall certainly was the most colorful of all of them. The other wizards had either stuck with natural colors, or with muted grays, tans, or beiges.

Xi Niu wondered why they all seemed to be glaring at him. What had he done wrong? What other secret, unspoken code had he just broken?

"Now, you need to reduce your wall back to its initial components," Gretchen announced. "While you may end up destroying some of the original pebbles, please try to leave at least half intact. I'll be measuring your success based on how the pebbles fill your original container."

Xi Niu groaned silently. This was going to be the hard part for him. As he'd been reminded twice recently, while he had power, he didn't have a lot of finesse. It would be easy for him to just pulverize the wall in front of him.

Delicately unraveling the spell that had created it, though, would take a lot more effort and concentration.

Xi Niu started in one corner, breaking it off and apart. But it crumbled to nothing in his fingers, dissolving into a fine plaster dust.

"Try washing out the colors first," Gretchen suggested quietly.

Xi Niu nodded. He hated to see the colors go, but he released them back into his imagination, until just a shadow of them remained on the white plaster walls, making them look dirty, as if shadows were stuck behind them.

He reached for another chunk of the wall, only to have it dissolve too.

Damn it! He wasn't doing this right.

Portals were so much easier. He just collapsed the tunnels he built instead of taking the chains apart one link at a time.

But maybe that was what was required here. Xi Niu tried to visualize the wall in front of him as a tunnel wall, those links connected together then flattened out. In his mind's eye, the solid wall transformed into a mesh of hundreds of chains running across.

There! There was a link he could get a hold of. He teased it open, then pulled it apart from the long chain on either side. Slowly, he pulled open additional links, letting them float free in the morass of magic.

The chains didn't dissolve into dust like the other chunks of the wall that he'd tried to take apart. Instead, they seemed to melt together, growing smaller and more compact.

Transforming back into pebbles.

Xi Niu learned quickly to just pick apart the center link of each chain, then one at the quarter and three-quarter marks. He didn't need to undo every link, just a few critical ones, and the chain would start to transform.

By the time he was finished, Xi Niu found his hands shaking and sweat dripping into his eyebrows. But he'd done it!

When he looked up, he realized that the rest of the class had left, and it was just him and Gretchen sitting there.

"I dismissed the class when I realized just how long you were going to take," she said.

"Did I pass?" Xi Niu asked. He couldn't help but feel discouraged for taking such a long time. But he'd managed to unravel his magic! A pile of pebbles sat in front of him, almost as big as the original one.

Gretchen reached over and scooped up the pebbles into their glass container. A line appeared on the side, the level at which the jar had been originally filled to.

The amount of pebbles he'd had left were just an inch below that original line.

"Yes, you passed," Gretchen said. "Though you took the long way to do this exercise," she chided. "First transforming the wall into metal chains? That was a powerful transformation. I had no idea there was that much trace metal in the pebbles. But it also took a lot of time. Why metal chains?"

Xi Niu shrugged. He knew he couldn't tell her that it was what he used to build portal tunnels with. "I'm familiar with them," he finally said.

"Then your assignment is to learn other forms," Gretchen said firmly.

"Yes, ma'am," Xi Niu said meekly.

He didn't have to be an ox all the time, bound in metal. Those chains weren't all that he held in his soul.

They couldn't be.

ONCE XI NIU knew to look for metal chains, he saw them in everything. Every part of magic that he did had chains connected to it. In addition, if he was being fanciful, he'd swear that he saw chains now connecting him to Ao Dan, to Kan Li, to the *Huli* HQ building itself. He wasn't sure if that was good or bad, or if it was just a thing.

He knew that it would take more strength than even he had to break all of them apart.

Maybe *Huli* Transport did already own his soul.

The following week, Bian Shay moved from her parent's house to an apartment down close to where she worked, complaining about the commute time and how this would make her life so much easier.

Xi Niu understood that he'd rarely, if ever, have the opportunity to see her again in the flesh. She'd probably been warned away, just as he had been.

His stubborn ox nature considered pestering her, trying to call her and speak to her. He'd been so looking forward to one of his friends actually being magical! In the end, he let her go. The chains that connected him to his friends were already weakening, the links breaking apart.

It surprised Xi Niu when his uncle showed up for dinner that Friday night. He arrived carrying boxes of take-out food, including Xi Niu's favorite stir-fried rice from the restaurant near *Huli* HQ. Jing Po had obviously arranged the gathering with his parents. No one had bothered to tell Xi Niu about it.

His uncle, his parents, and his sister all crowded in

around the table in the kitchen, sharing dishes and laughing. These were the times that reinforced the chains around Xi Niu, connecting him to his family. He held onto them desperately, afraid that they'd vanish as soon as he stopped paying attention to them.

Jing Po asked Xi Niu to walk with him to the curb and wait with him while the private car his uncle had hired came to pick him up.

The night was clear for once, though the neighborhood lights were too bright for the stars to shine through the darkness. The air still smelled wet, and Xi Niu wouldn't be surprised to see more rain come morning. A cool wind blew through the quiet subdivision, bringing the distant whine of traffic on the automated freeways nearby, a noise that always soothed Xi Niu.

"I made some inquiries," Jing Po said as they drew closer to the curb.

Xi Niu nodded, understanding that Jing Po was talking about the detection spells.

"I will repeat to you exactly what I was told," Jing Po said. He stopped and pulled himself up straight, staring with those hard eyes directly into Xi Niu's. "To be able to call something, you must be able to detect it, first."

Xi Niu gasped. The implications were obvious. If upper management did have a way of calling a hitchhiker to a tunnel, they would probably have to use some sort of detection spell first.

"Whatever spell the Yamamoto Logistics wizards are using to detect a hitchhiker isn't real," Jing Po said. "Upper management would never let that sort of secret out. It's probably why the *Huli* wizards don't bother. The spell's a sham."

"But there's probably a real spell, that we're just not

taught," Xi Niu said. The wonderful dinner he'd just eaten turned sour and into a hard ball in his stomach.

"Never will be taught," Jing Po said. He sighed. "If something happens to me, know that I don't blame you. I've had a good run."

"What do you mean?" Xi Niu asked, panic starting to creep in. "Nothing is going to happen to you. Nothing!"

Jing Po shrugged. "You're probably right. I still have many years left. The company won't get rid of me yet." He shrugged again. "I'm probably just being paranoid."

"You can never be too paranoid," Xi Niu said automatically, a quote from one of his games.

Jing Po gave him a true smile. "Now you're learning. Goodbye."

He gave Xi Niu a formal bow as the car pulled silently up beside the curb.

"Goodbye, Uncle," Xi Niu said, bowing just as low in return.

As Jing Po left, Xi Niu felt as though the chains that connected him to his uncle were growing thinner. He understood that was Jing Po's doing, so that the company wouldn't be able to use Jing Po against Xi Niu.

No matter. Xi Niu had been named after an ox. And his new job title was Holder. He would surprise them all by just how stubbornly he could hold onto things.

FOUR

THE PILOT

JUSTIN MENTALLY STRETCHED his arms out, laced his fingers together and cracked his knuckles. He couldn't do it physically. While the cockpit of the little experimental spaceship might, just barely, have had enough room for him to stretch his lanky six-foot-six body out fully, the bulky EVA gloves he wore didn't give him enough freedom of movement.

That was okay. He was here. He was ready. He was *present* as that yoga instructor he'd once dated had always talked about.

He could do this.

He was aware of the failures that had gone before him. Two of them, in fact. The first wizard who'd completely bombed at finding the tunnel linking the two portals in space, even though supposedly he'd tested positive for "tunnel sensitivity" back on Earth. (Justin had his doubts. Guy was probably related to one of the upper muckety-mucks at *Huli* Transport and had been passed along, no matter how much skill he'd actually had.)

The second had made it into the tunnel, and had

traveled there a while, maybe thirty minutes or so. Then something had happened. They weren't sure what. But the spaceship had been there, traveling along, all normal, then suddenly it disappeared and went off the grid.

Not that there was an actual grid. There had been a lot of problems figuring out how to follow a ship once it entered a portal tunnel. Usual communications wouldn't work. Scrying didn't really work either. The best they'd managed was attaching a scrying spell to the pilot before they entered, but even that was dicey.

So Justin knew the risks, ranging from embarrassment to certain death.

He was also aware of the rewards.

Becoming the first pilot to steer a ship from Earth to Mars in the blink of an eye.

This prize had to be his.

JUSTIN WASN'T the strongest wizard around. He barely eked out enough power to keep him in the wizard ranks and not be forced into management instead.

Who wanted to deal with spreadsheets (or rather, spreadshits) and quarterly quotas when they could do magic every day instead?

He'd never forget the hip-looking chick approaching him that afternoon in the coffee shop, when he was supposed to be studying for finals that marked the end of his first quarter of college. He figured she'd been put up to it by her friends or something. No beautiful, modelesque Asian woman wearing motorcycle leathers would come up to him of her own free will.

That she was offering him, *him*, a job working for this

transportation company as a messenger still had to be one of the weirdest experiences of his life.

And that was saying something for a working wizard who regularly dealt with monsters, gods, and immortals.

He would forever be grateful to Chan Yi, though she hadn't been able to see how her new recruit had shone. She'd been killed during a delivery less than a year later. Justin had never learned the details, but the rumor mill had insisted that it hadn't been a hitchhiker or a portal accident.

One of the core tenents of *Huli* Transport was that it was *neutral.* The company would carry packages and messages to all sorts of beings, the lawful and the not so lawful. They didn't often make a mistake and send messengers into harm's way. Mistakes got made sometimes, however.

Losing a messenger during a delivery was frequently career suicide for a manager. Though wizards would accidently kill messengers due to a hitchhiker, that was just considered part of doing business.

Negotiating a bad contract, where the parties didn't act in good faith, might get a manager demoted back down to messenger.

Justin had quickly passed up the ranks from messenger to wizard. It had only taken two years, despite the fact that he was an Anglo in a primarily Asian company, and looked like a typical Californian surfer dude, with bright blond hair, soulful brown eyes, and tall, lanky features.

But then he got stuck. He had tremendous focus despite his laid-back appearance, which was one of the reasons why he'd advanced so quickly. If he could bottle that focus and sell it, he'd make a fortune, despite the fact that the market was already crowded with mental enhancers.

Sheer magical power seemed to be the issue for him.

Lots of plans and dreams and schemes. Not enough magical strength to follow through.

Then again, if he had the power to accomplish something, that might mean he'd actually have to grow up.

And Justin had no intention of doing that. Like, ever. No matter that he was in his thirties now.

So he did just enough to get by, to stay a wizard. He'd even invested in nice suits and ties and always looked the part, keeping his blond curls cut close to his head. He'd learned quickly how the corporate game was played and followed the rules accordingly.

That didn't mean he ever had to play the game with his heart and soul, unlike some of his compatriots.

Justin spent his off time racing. He'd fallen in love with dune buggies as a kid, watching silly cartoons about talking cars who raced each other when their owners were away.

Like most magicians, Justin could see through the simulators. None of the VR training had worked for him. He had to practice in real time, on a long strip of beach that had at one point been privately owned. It was a pain in the ass to get to, using public transportation, and it wasn't until much later that Justin could afford an automated car service.

Still. Justin loved to drive, particularly when going incredibly fast, with the wheels spinning out on the sand and the ocean by his side. Taking those corners sharply, risking rolling his ride, just so he could have that burst of adrenaline as he crossed the finish line first.

When the opportunity had come up to become a spaceship pilot on the company's dime, he'd jumped at the chance.

Sure, he wasn't the strongest wizard. But he was the only one who drove himself on a regular basis. Who raced. Who had that laser focus.

He could do this.

JUSTIN FACED the monster of a tunnel in front of him. He felt as though he was a spear, poised to strike at the heart of a soulless beast.

The darkness of the abyss filling the dancing gray oval portal might intimidate some, especially the way the blackness sucked at his sanity and seemed to chitter at the back of his skull.

He told himself that it was no worse than facing off against his greatest racing rival knowing that his brakes were squishy and not as sharp as they should be. That just made it more of a challenge.

He could do this.

He ran through the "take off" checklist verbally with the controllers waiting in the much larger spaceship behind him. What he drove that day in no way resembled a dune buggy. It was a flat, long box, with the engines at the back, not rounded and bubble-like. Totally different aerodynamics, though one didn't really care about that kind of stuff in space.

Still, he'd absolutely add bright red racing fins to the outside of the spaceship if he could. Maybe a spoiler, too.

The engines only revved in his mind, a deep, rumbling sound, as he prepared himself. They'd modified the controls of a standard spaceship considerably. Instead of having a console with buttons on it, he had two sticks with levers on them, not quite paddle shifters but close. It was modeled on a fighter pilot's console because the company assumed that the pilot would need more control.

Despite the EVA suit, he smelled the familiar excitement sweat that always came when he was about to do something crazy. That he did crazy things often enough that he could identify that scent probably said something about him. Something he didn't need a shrink to tell him about.

This first tunnel wasn't that long. The two portals had

been built in sight of one another. Though the portals on Earth had been built standing side by side, these stood back to back. Justin assumed that was for his benefit, for him to conceptually visualize a straight tunnel instead of something that curved around. The experience would be the same, or so he'd been assured.

Straight through to the second star to the right.

After revving the engines one more time in his mind, Justin slid the sticks forward.

Passing through the first portal was an odd experience. Though his heavy spacesuit supposedly kept his inner temperature steady, he still felt a chill pass through him. His mom would say something about someone stepping over his grave, a saying that had never made sense to him. Particularly once he discovered that while magic was real, ghosts weren't.

Then he was in blackness. Utter, total darkness. There was nothing beyond the shell of his ship. No light, no sound, no life.

Just an abyss.

Justin pushed out his awareness, finding the edges of the tunnel easily. He made sure to aim his ship through the center of it, pushing forward slowly.

That chittering sound he'd heard before grew much louder. He knew it was the abyss scrabbling to sink its claws into his soul.

He wasn't about to lose this race just because of some stupid monster that didn't really exist.

Justin *focused*. He drove forward, redlining the engines. There wasn't that much distance between the two portals. It was *not* actually taking him this long.

Seconds, minutes, hours? ticked by.

He suddenly understood why the wizard who had tried this before him had failed. She'd driven herself out of the tunnel and directly into the abyss because she couldn't stand the insanity of the non-human space that surrounded her.

The pressure for him to do the same was building. He might be a wizard, but he was still human, still had a delectable soul.

Justin knew, he *knew* that he couldn't blink. He had to keep his eyes peeled for any hazard, though he couldn't imagine what might lurk in a magical tunnel strung between two portals.

However, staring into that blackness would put a stain on his soul that he'd never be able to scrub off.

Worse, it might demand that he grow up.

Justin took a deep breath. Then another. Sweat built up across the small of his back.

This was crazy.

Which was just like him.

Justin closed his eyes.

He instantly felt better. The pressure from the blackness surrounding the ship lessened.

He could do this.

He felt for the edges of the tunnel, correcting himself as he'd started to drift down and to the side. He retargeted himself down the center of the tunnel, easy and slick as a straightaway.

Now, he just had to *focus*. Keep himself and the ship on the path. Just a little longer.

Passing through the far end of the tunnel felt like exiting a bubble. Though Justin would swear he heard the *pop*, he was aware that chances were, it was just in his head.

"Yahoo!" he shouted. He wanted to do a victory lap, pushing and pulling at the controls, but everything felt sluggish, not just the levers but his arms as well.

"Justin, come in," came a voice over his comm. "Is that you?"

"Howdy!" he said, still feeling ecstatic. "That's me. Out on the far end of the tunnel."

The pause that followed his announcement seemed off.

"What is it?" he asked.

"It took you over three hours to make the trip," the controller said. "We'd considered collapsing the tunnel, but the scrying spell insisted that you were still alive."

Dang it! He *knew* that it had taken him much longer than the three minutes it should have taken.

"Can you redock with the main ship?" the voice said, sounding concerned.

What the hell? Of course he could!

Justin finally looked down at his control panel. Half the controls were black, scorched by an electrical fire he hadn't noticed. His power levels were falling. He was damned lucky his EVA suit was still functioning, or he might be as dead as his ship.

"Ah, negative," Justin said after pushing at his controls again, trying to get a response. "You're going to have to come get me, I'm afraid."

Despite the fact that his ship was a burned out mess, and that he still heard the skittering claws of the darkness at the back of his skull, Justin couldn't help but grin from ear to ear.

He'd made it. He'd done it. The first wizard to pilot a ship through a space portal.

He couldn't wait to do it again.

"WOULD YOU JUST LISTEN TO ME?" Justin said, exasperated. "You need shields or blast panels or something across the front windows to block out the tunnel. Any pilot worth their salt don't need to actually see to drive."

Jae Hwa, the engineer across from him merely shook her head. "That's counter intuitive." She was a serious woman in a serious job. She wore her long black hair down, hanging just to her shoulder blades. She had an oval face with flat cheeks, and her skin color was lighter than most of the people in the office, showing her mixed Korean-American heritage. She wore the standard white lab coat over a pretty pink blouse.

Justin felt like a dark cloud facing her. Instead of his usual laid-back T-shirt and jeans, he'd dressed in office attire: black suit, white shirt, and black tie. He was glad they were seated, as he knew that he'd be towering over the petite woman if they weren't. He'd learned early on to try to arrange meetings where he and his compatriots were sitting. Otherwise, he'd make whoever he was meeting with an instant rival just by towering over them. His pale looks did that already sometimes.

They faced off in a tiny conference room on Earth, at *Huli* HQ. Justin had never expected to become so familiar with the engineering floor. Not only did he know which vending machines offered up the sweetest coffee, he could also identify each of the conference rooms by smell alone.

This one always smelled like sweat, as if this were where managers took unfortunate underperforming scientists and lab rats and put the heat on.

"Driving a spaceship through a portal tunnel isn't necessarily the most intuitive task in the world either," Justin said. "Just—trust me on this one. It's why the other pilots have failed."

After Justin's success, the company had tried sending two other wizards through the portals. Justin had debriefed, and debriefed, and even agreed to a type of hypnosis so that his full experience could be recalled.

Which hadn't helped his nightmares about the abyss *at all*, though that wasn't something he was about to bring up.

That he'd closed his eyes had seemed particularly insane to one and all. The other pilots hadn't been willing to follow his example.

And both of them had died as a result.

The rest of the shielding on the ships had grown much more robust. After testing the latest model, he was actually able to drive away at the far end of the tunnel.

That didn't mean Justin was about to trust it. Particularly when these idiots wouldn't listen to him when it came to the blast panels across the windows. At least they had listened to him and had developed redundant electrical systems and engines.

However, no one, *no one*, could stare into the abyss for long. He suspected that Ao Dan's insane husband had done just that.

Justin was crazy enough, thank you very much. He didn't need to add to it. Though he suspected he already had, given how the abyss haunted him almost nightly…

"No one will voluntarily cut off their vision when they're flying a spaceship. And they know that the automated system won't work when it comes to piloting," Jae Hwa explained again.

"They have to," Justin said. "Can't you make it automatic? As part of the final checklist before a ship enters the portal?"

"Maybe," Jae Hwa said. "Though they won't appreciate us taking any control out of their hands."

Justin grimaced. He had to acknowledge the truth of that. He would hate it if the desk jockeys tried to dictate how he flew his ship. He'd probably find a way to rejigger their interference, overriding the nanny controls.

But they were losing so many pilots! Maybe some level of

automation would be worth it, if more pilots didn't end up dying.

Damn it! Was he actually growing up? Voluntarily giving up some of his freedom?

He was going to have to go and do something really crazy later on that night, just to make up for it.

"Can you build a two-seater ship?" Justin asked. "So that someone can actually fly along with me?"

Since he hadn't lost a ship (or himself) yet, after half a dozen trips through the portals, he hoped that the company might take a chance on killing two wizards at the same time.

"Yes," Jae Hwa said, nodding. "We've actually been working on a three-seater ship. That way, the seeker, the holder, and the pilot could all be traveling together."

That made sense to him. "Okay," Justin said. "Just let me know when I can go up again."

He still loved driving dune buggies. There was something about being on the beach, with the sand crunching under his boots and the gray ocean and the horizon so far off in the distance.

The thrill wasn't as great, though, not anymore. Fighting against sand seemed like a minor challenge to overcoming the abyss.

"We'll try out the two-seater spaceship next," Jae Hwa finally said after checking a few things on the tablet sitting on the table beside her.

"And the blast doors?" Justin asked.

"We'll consider your proposal," Jae Hwa said smoothly.

Justin huffed at her.

"It's the weight as much as anything else," she admitted. "We need to balance that out with the extra engines and redundant systems."

Justin would gladly give up an extra engine for more protection against the darkness. Before he could tell the engineer that, she swept out of the room, leaving him contemplating the balancing act he now appeared to be performing, between safety and insanity.

He suspected that the craziness would win out in the end.

But not before he managed to pound it into the skulls of his compatriots that the abyss was too much for anyone to stand.

JUSTIN COULDN'T HIDE his surprise when it turned out that his "co-pilot" for the next trip was none other than the wizard Ao Dan.

"Couldn't wait to try this yourself, eh?" Justin asked as he started going through the "takeoff" checklist, verifying that all systems were go.

"Something like that," Ao Dan said. He seemed shrunken in on himself. When Justin had been introduced to him back on Earth he would have said that Ao Dan was almost as tall as he was, if not in height, then in personality.

He'd even colored the outside of his EVA suit so it was scarlet and gold instead of gray and silver.

Justin might follow his example next trip.

This time, though, he needed to focus more on where they were going and what they were doing.

"Have you driven a spaceship before?" Justin had to ask.

Ao Dan gave him a crooked smile. "I've been studying along with the rest of the new pilots. I've taken a spin or two. However, like you, I have the advantage of having actually driven a car before."

"In this century?" Justin shot back. He was well aware of the reputation of the chaos wizard, of how ancient he was. He was surprised that the suits in charge had agreed to work with someone so far outside the mold. Ao Dan didn't even bother to fake it like Justin had.

Then again, he suspected that upper management had plans that would include Ao Dan's "accidental" death once the project was declared a success.

"I've driven recently enough," Ao Dan admitted with a shrug.

Justin grunted then continued on with his checklist. The panel in front of him had additional shielding on it, all the dials in a new configuration. The initial levers had turned into a more standard steering wheel, still with paddle shifters though. All the controls for directing the ship were at his fingertips.

As one of the last steps, Justin maneuvered the little ship to sit directly in front of the portal tunnel. Again, it appeared huge, much bigger than what he needed to drive a spaceship through. However, he also appreciated the larger size so that he wouldn't accidentally scrape against one of the sides of the tunnel.

"You ready for this?" Justin asked Ao Dan.

It took Ao Dan a moment before he turned his head to look at Justin. He blinked comically slowly. "Yes," he said, dragging the word out.

Damn it! This was not going to be good if Ao Dan was already under the influence of the abyss. What craziness would he try if he went insane?

Then Justin grinned. You know what? He was up for any craziness that the universe could throw at him. Would match and trump it.

"Let's go then. Hang on," he said, pushing the levers forward and driving the ship into the dark abyss.

THE FEELING of passing through a portal had never changed. It still gave Justin a serious chill. More than one of his nightmares involved ghosts dancing on his grave, pushing his dead and buried body deeper and deeper into the ground, toward the abyss that was growing just beneath him.

The engineers had assured him that the next ship would have blast doors covering the front windows. For this trip, though, he was just going to have to use his regular tHenry of closing his eyes.

As well as getting his passenger to do the same.

"Ao Dan," Justin said, gritting his teeth as he pushed the ship ahead. "Ao Dan!"

The wizard sitting beside him shook himself and finally looked over at Justin.

"You need to close your eyes now," Justin instructed.

To his surprise, Ao Dan complied. He gave a shudder, then turned back, his eyes still firmly shut, and faced forward.

"Good," Justin said. He closed his own eyes and drove forward as fast as he could go.

They'd learned that despite the fact that Justin always drove the ship at the same speed through the tunnel, the time it took varied. There was something about the nature of the tunnel itself that either impeded or speeded up the trip. It was part of that weird connection between physics and magic that the scientists were still figuring out.

The wizards who built the tunnel had learned to construct them in different ways. Justin had sat in on more than one debriefing listening to Xi Niu talk about how thin or thick the tunnel walls were.

Traveling to the moon now took thirty minutes, while a regular ship still took a few days. It was weird how the farther the distance between the two portals, the more stretched out and "thin" the portal tunnel grew, and the shorter the trip became.

"You doing all right?" Justin asked after some time had passed. He had no idea how much, as he couldn't open his eyes to check.

"I am," Ao Dan said after a moment.

"Is it what you expected?" Justin said, curious. He knew that the old wizard had envisioned a lot of the plan that they were now following, from the beacons to the ships.

"No," Ao Dan said immediately. "I can feel the edges of the tunnel. And you're staying right in the center, where you need to be. I wish I could have brought Henry up, so he could experience this."

"Henry, your husband, right? The guy who invented the beacons? Don't see why I can't fly him once as well," Justin said.

"He's dead," Ao Dan said. His words had a biting finality to them.

"I'm sorry for your loss," Justin said immediately. What else could he say? Though he'd never met the guy, Justin looked up to him. He'd invented the beacons and the future, after all.

Ao Dan took a deep breath. "He died last week," he admitted quietly.

"Whoa," Justin said. He couldn't help himself. He didn't think Ao Dan had taken any time off since then.

"I think that's the first time I've spoken the words out loud," Ao Dan said, his voice barely a whisper over the comm line. "I've just been getting used to the idea, you know?"

Justin didn't, but he nodded and said, "Yeah. Still. He created a great legacy."

"He gave the stars to mankind," Ao Dan said. His voice still sounded so sad. "I helped. But it also drove him insane."

Justin didn't want to ask, however, he had the feeling

suddenly that Henry hadn't gone quietly, that he'd possibly taken his own life.

"What are you going to do next?" Justin asked. He wasn't sure why. But it felt right, to get Ao Dan refocused on the future and not looking back.

The bitter laugh that he got in response didn't surprise him.

"I'd planned on bringing his ashes up here. To place them spinning into a tunnel," Ao Dan said.

"There is no way you're opening a hatch on this ship," Justin growled.

He couldn't risk opening his eyes and looking over at the other man, to see his reaction. He pressed on.

"You want to kill yourself, you go right ahead. Just not on my watch. Not on one of my flights. You aren't taking me with you, you understand?"

"Huh. I hadn't thought of it that way," Ao Dan said. "I really don't want to commit suicide," he added after a moment. "I have too many other things to live for. Like traveling out to the stars."

"Good," Justin said. "No more crazy talk about releasing something into a tunnel. You do that on your own time, in the future. Got it?"

"Loud and clear," Ao Dan said.

Finally, Justin could hear the smile in the man's voice.

"The scientists need to build better soundproofing in the ships," Ao Dan said after a few more moments.

"What do you mean?" Justin asked carefully. He'd only had to admit to hearing the scrabbling noise of the abyss scratching at the base of his skull that one time, under hypnosis. He'd never brought it up again.

"The abyss chitters now and again," Ao Dan said. "I've heard it before, talking to Henry. Don't you hear it?"

Justin took a deep breath before he decided to tell the truth. "I do. And it bugs me."

"They're the sirens of the abyss," Ao Dan said seriously. "They are trying to entice you to stay, so they can eat your soul."

Justin shook his head. "Not working," he lied.

Because really, why else would that noise follow him back to his nightmares? Besides to drive him crazy so that he'd actually join them in the abyss?

THE SCIENTISTS TINKERED with the shielding, finally finding the right combination of white noise and physical materials to block out some of the sound coming from the abyss. Justin was glad that Ao Dan had come along with him on the one trip through the tunnel. Despite being a chaos wizard and not part of the corporate hierarchy, he still had more pull than Justin and the scientists tended to actually listen to him.

The company had finally managed to recruit two other pilots who could handle a ship, as well as the tunnel itself. They both were grateful for the blast doors that covered the front windows, understanding that the pilot needed to fly by feel alone after their first trip.

Justin rejected the idea of putting additional cameras on the outside of the ship so that he could watch it as they traveled. Why would he want to see anything out in the abyss?

Finally, they were getting ready for the ultimate test, traveling from one beacon set up close to Earth to a second on Mars.

Justin wasn't sure how long it would take. The best

estimate was a few hours, given how travel through the tunnels grew shorter as the distance increased.

He prepared to endure the abyss that long the best he could, even taking a couple of days off and traveling to Hawaii, on the company dime, so he could bake his soul clean on the beach.

Not that he could ever fully erase the stain left by the abyss. He told himself that he was too stubborn to kill himself, though. He had plans. He was going to buy up the biggest beach he could, someplace warm, and race dune buggies all day long. He was racking up a ton of hazard pay by flying experimental spaceships, all of which he just socked away.

Planning that retirement brought him through even the worst of the nightmares.

Justin readied himself in his little spacecraft. The design had changed some, growing a bit rounder. Still not a dune buggy. And the bastards wouldn't paint racing stripes on the side. The back did kind of have a spoiler, now. Or at least he could call it that, though it was really just to vent the engine heat out of the ship and into space.

The extra shielding made the ship a lot heavier, so the engines had grown considerably.

Justin flipped down the shields before he entered the portal. He knew by feel exactly where he was going. He didn't want to see any more of the abyss than necessary. Just line himself up, and plunge forward.

The first portal seemed thicker than previous ones had. Instead of a single shivery moment, it felt as though it dragged on for over ten seconds at least. He wasn't sure why, but he'd have to remember to tell Xi Niu about it. Maybe the first portal just had to be more sturdy because the tunnel it was connected to was so much longer.

Though Justin did have recording equipment in the

cockpit, so he could speak out loud and automatically record his thoughts, he rarely did. He'd tried it a couple of times, but his voice had sounded so strained, so different than his usual, easy-going tones, that he couldn't bring himself to record more than what was absolutely necessary.

According to the completely mechanical clock mounted to the dashboard, he'd been traveling about fifteen minutes when a loud *whump* echoed through his tiny ship.

What the hell?

He regretted having vetoed cameras on the outside of the ship. Then again, what was there to see?

Skitter, skitter, skitter.

Oh shit. That sounded like claws scrabbling to get a hold on the back of his ship.

Though they'd discussed the possibility of hitchhikers jumping through one of the space tunnels, he'd never insisted on any sort of defensive weapons or shields. The scientists couldn't electrify the outside of the ship, as there was no guarantee that would even shock the creature who'd grabbed on. Might even feed the damned beast.

The entire ship shimmied, as if the creature going for a joy ride had just shaken itself like a dog.

Justin fought the controls, steering the craft back through the center of the tunnel.

Damn it! He didn't need this kind of excitement on this trip!

Though, to be honest, he kind of did.

How was he going to get rid of the hitchhiker, though? How could he fight it? He couldn't cast any magic at it. Magic was wonky, to say the least, in portal tunnels. Usually just didn't work, though when it did, it appeared to have a random effect. Suppose you were trying to call up a set of characters and create another portal inside the ship. Instead of a flaming character floating in midair, a rock might suddenly materialize. Or a bowl of petunias.

Could he scrape his unwanted guest off? Fly closer to the edge of a tunnel? Or would that be what the hitchhiker wanted, so that it could drag both of them through?

"I've got a hitchhiker," Justin announced. This was too important for him not to record. "Am trying evasive maneuvers to shake it."

The scientists hadn't wanted to put all the power and driving capability into the spaceships that Justin had asked for. However, they'd acquiesced to some of his demands.

That he'd taken the ship for a spin, literally causing it to do a somersault in midair, had seriously pissed them off. They had insisted that their spaceships didn't need that level of maneuverability.

Now, he could finally justify his requests.

Justin checked the sides of the tunnel, making sure that he was directly in the center. Then he flipped the ship over, going as quickly as he could. He didn't know if there was some sort of inertia that could be built up, that a hitchhiker would feel.

The way the thing outside shook the ship afterward just made Justin grin.

Didn't like that, eh?

He did a couple more flips. However, rolling the ship brought him too close to the edge of the tunnel.

Though he didn't have any visuals, and he couldn't *feel* the monster outside, he still knew it was there, breathing down his neck.

"Rolling and flipping the ship has pissed off the hitchhiker," Justin announced. "But I haven't been able to shake it."

Next, he purposefully flew higher in the tunnel, seeing if he could scrape off the hitchhiker.

That brought a lot more scrambling noises, as the creature appeared to move from the top to the bottom of the ship.

Warning lights suddenly blared on the console.

The exterior of the ship hadn't been punctured by claws. But something was now fouling the engines and the cooling vents in the back.

Damn it!

Stupid thing had moved away from both the top and the bottom of the ship and was now hanging off the back.

Justin pushed his engines to the max. He'd been in the tunnel at least two hours. How much longer?

The crunching noise that echoed through the ship made Justin break out in a sour sweat.

Seriously? Did that thing actually believe his ship was edible or something?

Or was it just so desperate to get at his soul?

He bounced the ship up and down, something else the scientists hadn't liked in the least.

But the crunching noise stopped.

Justin pinged back and forth, up and down, as much as he dared while still aiming for that finish line. He had to get there. He had to win! He had to be the first one to make the trip from Earth to Mars.

Just a little more.

The chittering noise at the back of his skull increased. It pressed against his skin, gnawing at his awareness.

"Shut up," Justin said through gritted teeth. There was no creature there. It was the abyss outside of the ship. Its siren call wanted him to turn the ship. Just a little. Just enough so he'd go through the tunnel wall.

Didn't he want to see what was out there?

Justin shook his head. The abyss had finally found his one true weak spot. How he clamored to be the first. He could do it, though no one else could. He could breach the tunnel wall and make it back alive.

The rational part of his brain knew better. It kept his focus on driving the ship forward, not allowing any more drift to occur.

Justin couldn't see the finish line. He could only feel it as he crossed, that long, drawn out *pop* as he slid into normal space.

Justin's fingers moved automatically, raising the blast doors over the front windows of the cockpit and spinning himself around.

Gods, the creature behind him was *ugly*. It had the snout of a boar with at least ten red, glowing eyes circling its skull. Its skin was corpse white, and it had eight matching arms, all tipped with deadly talons. It was easily half the size of the spaceship that Justin flew. Its legs were horselike, with powerful hindquarters and reversed knees. Looked like it would pack one hell of a kick.

Could he ram the thing? He knew he didn't have the magical strength to combat it.

Instead of the triumphant shout that he'd planned for successfully making his run, Justin called out, "May day. May day. Hitchhiker followed me through the tunnel." He looked down at his boards, pleased that all his systems had remained intact. Maybe he could simply run away?

The *Huli* Transport spaceship waiting for him on the other side of the tunnel spoke up. "We hear you," a deep woman's voice responded. "On our way."

Why they hell weren't they beside the portal just waiting for him?

Maybe now, though, the scientists would actually *listen* to him. They were going to have to arm the ships, so that when a hitchhiker followed him, he could at least blast it.

"Is that your hitchhiker?" the other ship asked as they drew up silently beside him.

"Well I'll be…" Justin swore.

The creature was imploding. Seemed that while it could survive the abyss, the cold vacuum of space had done it in.

"Damn thing was huge!" Justin said as the monster folded in on itself. "You've got to believe me." It was barely man-sized now, and shrinking rapidly.

A long silence followed his declaration. Finally, the woman's deep voice spoke again.

"We believe you," she said solemnly. "Looks like you've got claw as well as bite marks all over your rear."

Justin took a deep breath and relaxed abruptly.

Good to know that he wasn't completely crazy.

Yet.

JUSTIN HUNG out at the *Huli* space station orbiting Mars for a few days. The trip had taken only two hours and ten minutes, which was why the other spaceship hadn't been sitting there waiting for him. It hadn't maneuvered itself into place, yet.

He grew tired of the awed looks and hero worship much faster than he thought he would. Seriously. Was this part of growing up? It kind of sucked. He would have expected that he'd be able to live on that sort of praise.

Turned out, not so much.

He found himself voluntarily going and hanging out with the scientists and math geeks as they didn't appear to be overly impressed by him. They'd taken apart the rear end of his spaceship. He'd blanched when he saw just how huge the claw marks were. Damned thing had taken a bite out of the back as well.

The good news was that it hadn't been able to do much damage to the critical working parts of the ship. The bad news was that the scientists were going to have to rethink the design and figure out even better shielding.

Justin knew better than to believe it was because the company wanted to protect their pilots. Hell no. He'd seen the designs for the bigger cargo ships. *Huli* wanted to be able to guarantee delivery.

Fortunately, hitchhikers didn't appear that often. Maybe one trip out of one hundred. And it appeared that the creatures died as soon as they left the "haven" of the abyss.

Would there be creatures who didn't die? Justin was pretty sure there would be.

He was equally as certain that he never wanted to find out.

It was finally time for him to fly back. The scientists and engineers had rebuilt the rear end of his spaceship, once again rejecting his request for racing stripes.

While he could magically put them on the ship, he wasn't sure he was ready for that level of insubordination.

Today.

Justin hadn't bothered learning the names of most of the spaceships he flew. They were experimental models and changed so dramatically from one trip to the next that it didn't make sense to get too attached.

This was the first ship that he felt as though he'd actually flown twice. Plus, it had survived a monster's attack. He could learn her name.

Seemed that the engineers had named it *The Golden Peach*. Justin had looked up the mythological reference, learning that the immortals sometimes gifted humans with a golden peach so that they might live forever.

Made sense to him. Though he did shorten the name to just *Goldie*.

He went through the "takeoff" checklist with control, keeping *Goldie* turned away from the massive portal tunnel in front of him so that he didn't have to stare into the heart of the abyss just yet.

His hands shook as he went through the last few items on the list. Seemed that a hitchhiker had shaken his confidence some.

Justin turned *Goldie* square onto the portal tunnel as one of the last steps. He firmly closed the blast doors. The relief that washed over him didn't feel as great as it normally did.

Those tunnels were dangerous. He'd known that. Knew that. Accepted the challenge and the thrill of cheating death every time.

There was going to be a time when he didn't make it. When a tire would blow, or his engine, and there was no way of pulling over to the side to fix the machine.

Justin had to admit that chances were, his flying days were numbered. He could do this, here and now. He *had* to, had to get back onto that horse, right now, or else he'd never fly again.

He took a deep breath to steady himself. Then another.

"Is everything all right?" came a voice over his comm.

"Everything's fine," Justin lied, taking one last deep breath before plunging himself back into the darkness.

He could come through this one last time. He was enough of a grownup to do that.

JUSTIN FOUND himself straining to hear something, anything, out of the ordinary through the first part of the trip. He was jumpy. He tried to convince himself that he wasn't, that he could overcome his nerves.

He suspected he was lying to himself, however. Even after the first hour or so, he'd still remained on edge.

That level of stress wasn't good for him, and would eventually kill him if the abyss didn't get to him first.

Justin popped out the other end of the tunnel, orbiting Earth, in just over three hours according to the mechanical clock on the dashboard. He didn't know what factors had made the trip longer, whether it was the tunnel or the spaceship or the driver.

Or maybe a combination of all three.

Blinding light shone in through the windows when he opened the blast doors.

What the hell? They hadn't done something stupid like directed him at the sun, had they?

He was tempted to close the doors, but instead, turned the ship around, away from the bright source.

The light went out as quickly almost immediately.

"Control? What the hell was that?" Justin asked.

An unfamiliar male voice came over the comm channel. "Smile, son! You've just made history!"

"This is a private comm line," came control's smooth voice. "And you are violating company space."

"There are some things that are more important than your company's private space," the voice sneered. "Such as finding a wormhole that can be used to make the trip from Earth to Mars in just three hours. When were you planning on sharing that with the rest of the world? Or were you going to keep it secret forever?"

Justin froze. Oh, no. That was the press.

The first law about magic was that you never told anyone. Ever. Even if you did tell them, most mundanes couldn't see the magic you performed anyway.

Flying a spaceship through a portal tunnel, though…

That could be measured. Recorded. Even if the mundanes couldn't see the portals on either end.

He maneuvered *Goldie* around to dock with the larger spaceship, letting the arguments of the two wash over him. They didn't really matter.

Word was going to get out sooner or later. He knew that the company had been hoping for later, though.

And now that the cat was out of the bag, there was no way it was ever going back in.

Justin stayed in his ship for just a few moments longer. This was the end of his trips for a while he suspected.

Maybe for good, if he was being honest with himself.

No matter. He could grow used to teaching others to do what he did. And racing buggies to his heart's content.

As for the constant hero worship, well there were worse things than being famous. Right?

FIVE

THE COMPANY

FU RUI WALKED QUICKLY BACK to his office after the disastrous board of directors meeting, not bothering to stay and chat with any of the visiting foreign directors.

Fools.

Of course, he didn't allow any of his anger to show in his demeanor. He retained a pleasant half smile, nodding at people he passed. His somber, green-gray suit, white shirt, and golden brown tie looked impeccable, as always. Like the other directors, he regularly saw a beautician for facials and manicures, keeping his skin supple, his nails impeccable, his teeth white. Unlike the others, he didn't dye his black hair, though he did keep it cut in a traditional, short style. While the gray at his temples did mark him as older, it also gave him a more distinguished look, or so his wife had assured him more than once.

And as modern and "hip" as these directors all claimed to be, they'd been raised to honor their elders, and so the gray actually gave him more of an edge than they realized, though it was unconscious on their part.

Even after Fu Rui reached the sanctuary of his office, he

didn't opaque the glass windows looking in from the outside so he could express his anger. No, he maintained a cheery expression even as he called up his resignation letter.

It was only then that he hesitated. Yes, they were fools to think that the latest Chinese government regulation could be outmaneuvered. Sure, the company had enough clout (and could pay enough bribes) to do that initially.

But couldn't these fools see what was going to happen eventually? Over time, the government would tighten their hold. Even over wizards and magical training that their watchdogs couldn't actually see. The government would eventually insist on *Huli* Transport providing the guards, certified magicians. Then they'd crack down further, insisting that the wizards and messengers transfer their allegiance from the company to the country.

It was a pattern that Fu Rui had seen again and again. It was less prevalent in "modern" mainland China. People had more freedom now. That power creep would occur though, bringing with it the inevitable rot.

Then again, there was a reason why Fu Rui, despite being mundane, was on the corporate board.

While he might not have any magic, he could see patterns that seemed to elude the other managers and directors. More than once, they'd jokingly asked him to "look into his crystal ball" to find the answers.

What he saw disturbed him, but no one had been willing to listen that morning.

The board had been preparing their statements and demonstrations of space travel for the rest of humanity.

That thrice-damned news team who'd recorded Justin flying from Mars to Earth in just a few hours had beat them to the punch by several months.

Fu Rui was grateful that news hadn't leaked out earlier. Then again, the science behind the beacons was so new, so radically different, that it would be extremely difficult to reverse engineer. All the reports said that the signal that the beacons emitted wasn't detectable by any of the sensors that were currently in place, so it was likely that even if someone ran across one of them, they'd have no idea what it was doing, thinking that it did nothing at all.

No one who was a part of the program would talk, either. They were indoctrinated too thoroughly to admit to anything, even to the other wizards in the company.

However, the word was out now. And the fallout had been as nasty as Fu Rui had predicted.

He dismissed his resignation letter without signing it. He knew better than to do something so rash, particularly while in the heat of anger. Instead, he signed out of his computer, picked up his jacket, and left the office. It was midday. Let his secretary and the rest of them believe he was just going out to an early lunch meeting.

They didn't need to know that he wasn't coming back that afternoon. He could take some calls on his comm if he had to, if something came up. He'd cleared his afternoon earlier anyway, planning on spending time with the board members. Now, he was just taking the time off.

He needed a clear head to peer through the darkness surrounding the company's future, to predict the next step they needed to take.

He sent a message to his wife that he was coming home, hoping that she'd meet him there, then he stepped out of the fortress the office had become and into the chaos of reporters swirling on the street and sidewalk outside.

The shouts always surprised him. Did the reporters actually believe that he might talk to any of them? At least China still had rules about what a reporter could yell at someone. Unlike over in the United States, where slander laws had taken a definite step backwards, allowing the most outrageous things to be said as long as the "intent" was merely to get a reaction and not because the individual actually believed what they said.

His car slid up to the curb and Fu Rui slipped into the back without even looking at the reporters. He and his people still had some level of free movement, though he doubted it would last long, not given the latest edicts from the government. Drones would follow the car though the crowded streets of Shanghai, and would dutifully record him exiting the car and going into his house.

At that point, they'd be stalled. The infrared and X-ray abilities of news drones had been outlawed, though Fu Rui had no doubt that the government had drones capable of doing that sort of watching and listening.

Hopefully he hadn't given them enough cause to pay that much attention to him. Yet.

At least Fu Rui was with his people, as it were. Other corporate headquarters had faced ugly discrimination, as had a lot of Asians, in general. Stupid people had assumed that all Asians were alike, that they all had this secret technology that they were unwilling to share with the rest of the world.

Governments had been briefed on the fact that it was, in fact, magic and not technology.

A few had shared that knowledge with their citizens. Many had not.

But there was nothing Fu Rui could do about that either. Most people couldn't see or sense magic, even when it was performed right in front of them. The recordings of the spaceship showed it slowly disappearing as it went through an invisible door, then reappearing again the same way.

They hadn't gotten to the point of taking mundanes through the portal tunnels yet. Or goods.

All that was put on hold, at least for the past three weeks, while they dealt with the reactions of the world.

Fu Rui's comm chirped, letting him know that his wife was waiting for him.

He felt the first true smile of the day creep over his face.

Maybe she could help him find the right path through the darkness, as she was his one constant light.

———

FU RUI DIDN'T SWEEP his wife into his arms when he walked into their kitchen, though he wanted to. He wanted to feel her solid form against his chest, breathe in her sweet scent, bury his face in her hair and feel its soft silkiness against his cheek. She wore an elegant silk dress, green with a pattern of tiny brown leaves on it. A solid sheath covered her torso, while gauzy sleeves ran from shoulder to wrist.

Instead of grabbing her, Fu Rui gave her a very formal bow when he walked in, saying, "*Konichiwa, Umeko.*"

He only ever called her by her given name at home. Outside, he only ever referred to her by her Chinese name, Ya Dei. Most people had no idea of her background, her mother having been brought to China as a wife for an important official. No one at the company, certainly, had a clue of how she'd been raised.

Umeko returned his bow gravely. "That bad, eh?" she asked as she reached for the plates and started serving the plain noodle dish she'd had delivered, made out of buckwheat noodles, with a sweet brown sauce and freshly cooked eel.

Fu Rui merely grimaced. She served him, then herself. They both ate in silence, the quietness of the house restoring Fu Rui's equilibrium. He knew people, like his brother, who wanted constant noise in the background. The quietness of Fu Rui's house disturbed his sibling.

It soothed Fu Rui's soul like nothing else.

Only when they'd both finished their plates and Umeko had poured them both full cups of green tea did Fu Rui speak.

"Come sit with me?" he asked, holding out his hand.

Umeko gave him her free hand as well as a smile.

He brought the back of her soft hand up to his lips for a quick kiss, drinking in her warmth and serenity. Then he led them to the back living room.

The front living room, like the kitchen, had been built to impress when they entertained guests. The rooms contained all the modern conveniences, with expensive furniture and fixtures. They'd moved to this showcase only after their two boys had entered university, both of them completely mundane, like their parents.

The back living room, part of the private areas of the house, was tiny and cozy. Both Fu Rui and Umeko had a comfortable reading chair there, made out of old-fashioned cushions instead of modern form-fitting gel. An artificial fireplace took up most of one wall, though the glowing embers and flames were designed to warm the room.

Behind the two chairs, on the wall opposite the fireplace, was a loveseat. It was covered in a soft purple material, and the perfect size for the pair of them to curl up together on. A low coffee table stretched out in front of the loveseat.

Fu Rui put down his cup of tea, then sat, stretching his arm out, inviting Umeko to curl up beside him.

She did so immediately, resting her head against his shoulder, drawing her feet up under her.

He indulged himself and took a deep breath of her sweet scent, letting the warmth of her body pressed up against his side seep in.

"Want to tell me about it?" she asked quietly, still sipping her tea.

'The fools of the board still think that we'll be able to

continue to operate as we had been," Fu Rui admitted. "That the government won't tighten their grip. That we'll be immune, somehow, to their regulations."

"The company is immune in many ways," Umeko pointed out. "They can't regulate the business parts that they can't see."

"That's what the board said. But it's only a matter of time before the government insists that we provide the observers."

Umeko nodded. "And you don't trust that the wizards will stay true to the company, right?"

"Correct," Fu Rui said. Umeko, as always, saw through to the heart of whatever problem he was having.

"Do you want to keep the company intact?" Umeko said after a moment of contemplation, sipping her tea.

Fu Rui took a moment and a drink from his own cup. "I do," Fu Rui said. "We can't spin off the mundane arm of the shipping company, though that might split the government's attention and give us a little more time. However, the future has the magical and the mundane welded together. While it might make sense to separate the two parts currently, it would be a horrible solution for the long term."

Umeko turned and kissed his cheek softly. "That's just one of the things I love about you, you know? That you always try to take the long-term approach."

"Thank you," Fu Rui said. Being too focused on the current quarter's profits had always been something the company discouraged. Any new manager who was hired on was always given long sessions of history lessons over the course of their first year so that they'd understand why short-term thinking had led the United States to lose as much power as it had.

How far it had fallen.

As much as *Huli* Transport tried to indoctrinate its employees, teaching them that the company came first, human nature was still greedy. It was easier to control on the magical side of things—a manager who signed a bad contract, promoting greed before messenger safety, could be demoted in such a way as to put their life at risk.

The punishments weren't as severe on the mundane side. Mistakes were made more often, and were more tolerated. Tying bonuses to company profit, not department level, helped.

Once again, Fu Rui regretted the lack of restrictions placed on the board. If he had more power, he could maneuver around these idiots. However, additional restrictions would have tied Fu Rui's hands and he wouldn't have been able to jam through all the funding he'd needed to get their space program up and running.

Fortunately, they didn't have the nonsense of being public, unlike an American company. They didn't answer to shareholders about the huge loss they were going to appear to take this year as they ran through the several billion dollar "nest egg" they'd accumulated.

They did, however, answer to the government, who wanted its dirty fingers in their pie.

"Thinking long term," Umeko said after another comforting moment, "means the consideration of taking the company someplace else. Leaving the mainland."

Fu Rui sighed. "I know," he said quietly. They'd had variations of this conversation every time a major crisis had occurred. However, before this, Fu Rui and his predecessors had always waited. Even through the disastrous wars, first with Russia (which they technically could say they'd won, having gained so much more territory), then with India (which was a draw, as neither of them had taken more land, and instead, just lost a generation of men who never could have married in the first place).

Yet more war loomed, though not on the Asian

continent. The latest disagreement had started between the South American countries, but they were determined to bring in as many foreign nationals as they could. *Huli* Transport had hardened the offices they had in every major city in South America when the conflict had begun.

The company had had to temporarily close some of the offices when word got out about magic and a literal wizard hunt had started.

"The board will never agree to move the primary headquarters," Fu Rui said. "They won't agree to incorporate anywhere other than mainland China." There had been serious talk about moving to the United States over two hundred years before, however, the depression that the US entered into a few years later had tabled those talks.

"Do you need the board's approval?" Umeko asked.

Fu Rui blinked, surprised. "What do you mean?" he asked. He'd never thought about just taking the company someplace. Was that even possible?

"You're in charge of the future of the company," Umeko said. "That's always been your unofficial job title. The space program. *Huli* Intergalactic. Most of that is already taking place in the United States. Can't you sever off that chunk and just go?"

"That's the same as separating off the magical from the mundane portions of the company," Fu Rui said.

"Not necessarily," Umeko said. "You'd still need parts of both the shipping aspects of the company, as well as the magical parts. You would no longer be part of the messaging portion, though."

"Who's to say that the gods and the immortals won't want intergalactic deliveries?" Fu Rui said in response. No, he really didn't want to split the company up, not unless that was the only way to ensure that they survived.

"True, they might," Umeko said. "So in your ideal world,

you'd dissolve the Chinese corporation, reforming the company as a brand new entity, in another country? With guarantees of non-interference?"

"Yes," Fu Rui said. "Exactly."

"Where?" Umeko asked. "The United States?"

"No," Fu Rui said almost immediately.

That seemed to surprise her. "Why not?"

Fu Rui gave a sigh. "I know it makes logical sense. The United States is still a powerful nation. They've solved a lot of their previous problems, like healthcare and homelessness, as well as livable wages." It had taken what had amounted to a civil war in order to get those issues resolved, but they finally had.

"But?"

"But Americans have more of a sense of self-identity," Fu Rui admitted after a moment. "In the short run, *Huli* Transport would do very well on American soil. In the long run, the company would decay and collapse, implode if you will, because the employees would not give their allegiance to the company as they would need to."

No matter the consequences, managers in the US branches of the company still made more mistakes, negotiating with beings who acted in bad faith. The European countries had less of a problem, but their failure rate was still higher than the Asian countries.

Umeko nodded, then finished her tea and set her cup down. "Then where?"

Fu Rui smiled at her. "We'll move the company to Japan," he said quietly.

Umeko gasped. "Really?" she asked, stunned.

She knew very little of where her mother had come from, just from videos and VR. Japan had also suffered through several depressions, their economy imploding as their birthrate plummeted. Like the Chinese, the Japanese didn't want to marry outside of their genome, as it were.

They'd been forced to innovate, as only the Japanese could.

People who had a significant portion of Japanese heritage in their genes were paid huge bounties for moving back to Japan and having children within a specific number of years. They'd passed laws, ensuring that the more children those sorts of couples had, the lower their taxes and the more concessions they had.

While critics in the rest of the world had predicted that bringing in so many foreigners despite their lack of genetic purity would ruin Japanese culture, they hadn't understood the essential nature of Japan. So many cultures and traditions had already washed over the island over the centuries. The Japanese had a way, though, of absorbing all those new ideas and traditions, then transmuting them so they became uniquely Japanese.

"The Japanese have a business culture like ours," Fu Rui said. He'd already thought through all of this, but it was good to speak it out loud. Umeko would be able to find any gaps in his logic. "They will ensure that the individual continues to put the company first. Even if the company itself loses some of its Chinese identity. It would survive."

"Is that the only reason?" Umeko asked with a sly smile. She knew there must be other reasons that he would have up his sleeve.

"We have a very strong branch there," Fu Rui said. "Second only to the US office. The Japanese government would throw money behind the space program, just so they could say that they'd been there first. Plus, the government interference would be much less, at least in the current incarnation of their government."

"And?" Umeko said after a moment.

"And there's a rival company based there," Fu Rui admitted. It was actually the primary reason why he'd eventually settled on Japan. "Yamamoto Logistics."

Umeko blinked, surprised. "Rival how?"

"They were formed by a non-human," he said, not wanting to go too far into the weeds. "They've dealt with beings that *Huli* Transport, on general principle, never did. Not because they weren't trustworthy, but because they were poor. They couldn't pay us. Yamamoto Logistics started off with a barter system, not cash based."

"Interesting," Umeko said, obviously fascinated. "But why would you want to move to Japan if that's the home of your greatest rival?"

Though he hadn't said anything about their position, he was pleased that she'd picked up just how much of a rival the other company had become, how much they'd started eating into *Huli* Transport's magical arm of the business.

Fu Rui turned on the seat so he could face his wife straight on. "We can't move the company, the board would never agree to it. Not only because they don't want to leave Chinese soil, but because they don't want to lose their own cushy positions of power. However, what would happen if the company received a hostile takeover bid? That they can't fight off?"

"Is that even possible?" Umeko asked. "With a privately held Chinese company?"

Fu Rui gave her a large grin. "I can make it so."

FU RUI and three other board members whom he trusted to stay quiet flew to Japan on a private corporate jet. They couldn't travel secretly, there were no secrets from today's governments. The company had enough clout still to ensure they wouldn't be detained either going or returning. And since Fu Rui was a mundane, he couldn't travel using a portal, not unless he was fully encased in a portable "coffin"—and he didn't trust anyone enough to go to that extreme.

The negotiations took four long, hard days of work. Fu Rui and the others practically lived in the conference room that had been set aside for them and the upper management of Yamamoto Logistics. Every evening, they'd gone to one private teahouse after another, drinking with their counterparts, getting to know each other on a more personal level, as was required by social niceties. Afterward, they'd take "clear out" drugs that weren't completely legal to wash the alcohol out of their systems and meet for another hour or more, discussing strategies and logistics. (The drugs had too many potential side effects, such as heart attack, for them to be completely legal in a form that was actually effective.)

After a few hours of sleep, they'd meet and start the process all over again. Fu Rui knew his body wouldn't last long on the stims, that eventually he'd crash and burn and be sick for more than a week. He had no choice, though, and was trying to cram in as much as he could before the inevitable.

The windows of the conference room overlooked downtown Tokyo. The Japanese had taken their design cues from the most cutting-edge films, so the city was flooded with neon, three levels of trains traversed between the tall buildings, and the people, though covered in glitz, retained a solid, steady core of calm underneath.

Mr. Sato joined Fu Rui at the window during one of the breaks. They were putting the final touches on the agreed compromises.

There were some things, however, that Fu Rui wouldn't budge on.

Namely, the name of the parent company.

Both *Huli* Intergalactic and Yamamoto Logistics would be separate entities, with bylaws that would make it difficult for either one to take over the other.

Fu Rui insisted that the parent company would still be called *Huli* Transport. Or else he would leave and the merger papers would never be finalized.

The wizards on Fu Rui's team assured him that while Mr. Sato was a wizard, he was a manager, and not that powerful. His true strength lay in his charm, which worked even on Fu Rui to some extent.

They both wore gray suits that day, Mr. Sato's a shade lighter, both cut out of incredibly expensive fabric and impeccably fitted.

Fu Rui knew that Mr. Sato, or Isamu, or even Sam as he'd liked to be called when he'd had too much saki, was as frustrated as he was.

"Beautiful, eh?" Isamu said after a few moments of staring out at the technicolor landscape.

"It is," Fu Rui said, nodding. "Shanghai is also beautiful like this. More bHenry, less plastic, though," he added, teasing.

Isamu gave him a great grin. "More traditional, old-fashioned," he teased in return.

They had poked at each other in this vein for much of the negotiations, using variations of "stodgy and out-of-date" versus "soulless and modern."

"You will eventually give in," Fu Rui warned after a few moments of companionable silence.

"Really?" Isamu said. He gestured with his hand. Fu Rui couldn't feel it, couldn't see it, but still knew that the man had just performed magic. If he had to guess, the magic would isolate them from the rest of the room and their conversation wouldn't be overheard by the others.

"Why do you think that we will give in?" Isamu asked. "It is a name. You need us more than we need you. Why is this such a sticking point?"

"Names are important," Fu Rui said. "You know that."

Isamu nodded. Myths about the power of using the proper name for things were just that, myths. However, they both understood the psychology as well as the marketing strength behind such choices.

"Changing the name would be one step too far for the other members of the board," Fu Rui said. "Even when faced with the inevitable, they'd fight, just because of the name."

Isamu shrugged. "I feel certain that you could get around such disagreements if you needed to."

"*Huli* Transport existed long before Yamamoto Logistics," Fu Rui continued. "It's a name that even the gods trust."

"They are learning to trust us more," Isamu said. "We would take a hit for changing the name, that is true. But our services are invaluable. Any client who left due to such a trifling matter would come back."

"You're wrong," Fu Rui said. "If we divide our clientele, fracture it, other competitors would come in. We would never be able to solidify our base again."

Isamu sighed. Fu Rui had given all these arguments before, laid them out precisely. "What is the real reason?" he insisted.

Fu Rui gave a mirthless laugh. "What can I tell you that you'd believe? That it's ego on my part? That the wizards won't switch allegiance easily and you'd lose half the employees that you'd hoped to gain? That the gods have whispered in my ear that it must be so?"

"Have you met any of the immortals? Gods? Beings of power?" Isamu said, curious.

It was Fu Rui's turn to shrug. "Supposedly. I have no

memory of it, though I've been assured that it's happened." As a mundane, any visit from a higher being was immediately forgotten. No one could explain why that was how it worked, but all the experts agreed that was indeed the process. Only someone with magical power would remember such a meeting, and only if the gods willed it to be so.

Isamu nodded. "While I don't want to let go of this point, my gut says that I must. I think you have been touched by the gods, in order to foresee what you do."

Fu Rui shook his head. "No, it's merely study and analysis." He'd never been tempted to give credit for his abilities to some figure outside of himself.

"As you say," Isamu said. "Study and research. Though also a touch of luck."

Fu Rui raised an invisible glass, toasting Isamu. "To luck."

"To luck."

THE GOVERNMENT RAID surprised everyone except Fu Rui, who'd predicted that would be one of the next steps taken by a leadership desperate to show their power even over such exotics as wizards and magicians.

Fu Rui hadn't bothered to warn anyone, however. He suspected that some of the directors had known, probably tipped off by their contacts at the local law enforcement offices.

He stood to the side and let his computer, his files, everything be confiscated. The important documents had already been relocated to a hidden safe. Fortunately, there was too much for the officers to grab that was in clear view and easy reach for them to start tearing apart the walls, searching for hidden compartments.

At least during this visit.

Only after the disastrous raid had finished, leaving the offices looking as though a powerful cyclone had gone through, disrupting desks and scattering papers, did Fu Rui bother meeting with the rest of the board of directors. He'd personally seen to it that they would have a quorum of voting members on hand today.

The board finally appeared to have woken up to the consequences of the government edicts. How the company would lose the allegiance of the wizards, particularly when the managers had no power when it came to getting the wizards out of questioning or even prison.

Plus, there was that clause in the bylaws about never allowing a hostile body to take over the corporate identity. The raid had ruthlessly driven that point home. The current government would take over the business either with their cooperation or not.

The choices the board faced were either to accept the merger Fu Rui presented them or dissolve *Huli* Transport for good, scattering the wizards and their people to the winds.

"It is a bitter pill to swallow," Fu Rui admitted as he passed out the merger papers. "But it's the only way the company will survive. And the company *must* survive."

He knew that not all the board members agreed. Some had too much ego, and were focused on their own, private legacies, not the greater good.

"It is our duty, not just to the company, but to the gods themselves, to ensure that *Huli* Transport remains *neutral*. I need not remind you of the vows you all once took upon entering service here," Fu Rui continued. "And with the sort of government interference that's coming, we would most certainly be forced to break that most solemn of vows."

A collective sigh went through the proud men and women gathered around the table. They all knew. And they knew the consequences of what would happen if they lost that neutrality.

Huli Transport would be no more. The gods themselves had assured them of this.

One by one, they all agreed to the merger, to gulping down that bitter draft, agreeing it was better to survive elsewhere than to stay on the mainland and fight.

"You've done the right thing," Fu Rui said as he collected the papers, making sure that they'd all been activated to not only record the signer's signature but also their thumb print and verifiable DNA.

He couldn't feel happy about such an outcome, though it had all been his maneuvering that had brought it about. Including a word or two placed in the ear of the local law enforcement offices, about how the company would be vulnerable to such a raid.

He might have felt some satisfaction, perhaps.

Mostly, he felt tired.

He couldn't rest, though. He had more work to do.

THAT AFTERNOON, Fu Rui managed to sleep on the plane over to the US. It was a long enough journey that he should have been able to relax the entire way, but that was impossible.

Umeko had already immigrated to Japan. As had their sons. The company was well on its way, the wizards and messengers on both side working overtime in order to transfer everything from one location to the other, away from mundane channels and government spying eyes, portals going practically nonstop.

There were still loose ends to be cleaned up, though.

The young holder, Xi Niu, waited beside the corporate car at the airport, as Fu Rui had requested.

The power the young man held was not obvious. He had a slim build, and his face had a pinched look to it, as if he hadn't been satisfied with his last meal. His suit was ill-fitting despite being made from a good black wool. He bowed his head and opened the door for Fu Rui, before sliding in and sitting beside him.

"Do you know why I asked for you?" Fu Rui said as soon as he verified that the glass separating the driver from the passengers was closed and the soundproofing activated.

Wouldn't stop a wizard's scry spell, but he figured Xi Niu would warn him if they were being followed that way.

The young man shrugged. "First guess would be bodyguard. But I suspect you want something else in addition to that."

Fu Rui nodded. Despite his lack of magical finesse, and for having that lumbering, ox quality despite his slim size, Xi Niu wasn't stupid.

"I have received assurances of your loyalty," Fu Rui said slowly. "That you'll remain loyal to the company."

The boy grimaced but he nodded. "I'm aware of the consequences of disloyalty," he said.

Fu Rui wasn't sure what the young man meant, but now wasn't the time or place for such discussions. "Were you aware that other members of your team may not have been as loyal?"

Xi Niu's eyes stared out into the distance for a moment. "I wasn't," he said slowly. "But I have a guess. Ao Dan?"

Fu Rui nodded. "That news team didn't just show up by accident." It had taken quite a bit of tracking, but he was fairly certain that Ao Dan had tipped off the news, making sure that they had two teams in place and could record Justin's ship both entering as well as leaving the portal.

They actually had been recording for a while, and had marked more than one ship coming and going between the portals. They didn't bother saying anything until the big trip had been successful.

"What are you going to do?" Xi Niu asked. He sounded curious.

Fu Rui was aware of Ao Dan's great power, as well as the fact that the man was a warlock, not a wizard, and his ultimate loyalty ran to himself and none other.

"I'm just here to listen to what he has to say," Fu Rui said.

"And me?" Xi Niu said, sounding more worried now.

"You're here to make sure that he listens in return."

FU RUI COULDN'T SAY what exactly happened when the two wizards met. He hadn't felt any sort of great wind or heard any explosions. He wondered if there had been plenty of both, though, as the rest of Ao Dan's apartment looked as if it had gone through a worse storm than the offices had. He'd been present during most of the fight, but the memory of it was already fading, changing, until he'd remember nothing but standing there in the aftermath.

Ao Dan now stood in front of him, held stiffly at attention by Xi Nui. The wizard wore the most outrageous purple jumpsuit with constantly changing patterns of silver sequins. Scorch marks burned the floor around him. Fu Rui almost wished he could have seen the pyrotechnic show.

"It has come to my attention that you tipped off the news teams about the beacons and our progress," Fu Rui said mildly.

"I'm not bound by your rules," Ao Dan sneered at him.

"True," Fu Rui said. "I understand that the terms of the

agreement between us never specified your silence in the matter. I think they just assumed that you weren't going to go blabbing about it to all and sundry."

Though Xi Niu held Ao Dan firmly, the chaos wizard still managed a slight shrug.

"What I want to know is why," Fu Rui said. "Why alert the media? Why give them footage? Why let everyone know before we were ready?"

"You were ready," Ao Dan said. "Justin had completed the run not only from Earth to Mars, but from Mars back to Earth. The project was a success. We can travel to the stars, now."

Fu Rui pressed his lips together instead of replying right away. No one could just fling themselves across the galaxy at this point. There were still experiments that needed doing, tests that needed running. They knew how to bring a mundane through a portal, by using a sort of coffin and floating it through with a messenger. It didn't work every time, though, and there was always the chance of hitchhikers.

There needed to be a lot more experiments with how to "package" mundanes and carry them through the beacon portals as well.

"Even though I disagree, with you, I still don't understand why you felt the need to expose us this way," Fu Rui said. "Was it always part of your plan? Was it just to sow more chaos? Were you directed to do it? Why?"

"I didn't trust you," Ao Dan said after another moment. "There was too good of a chance that the company would have kept the knowledge all to themselves for years. Maybe decades."

"Why would we do that?" Fu Rui said, confused. "Once the program was established, we would have announced it."

"I don't believe you," Ao Dan said, anger tinging the edges of his voice.

"Do you not understand how much profit we'll make? We'll be able to guarantee a short delivery time for all goods between the planets," Fu Rui said, still perplexed. Surely Ao Dan had been around long enough to understand a motive such as money.

"And who's going to pay for the company to continue its work?" Ao Dan shot back. "The Chinese government?"

Fu Rui took a deep breath. Was that at the root of Ao Dan's discontent? The latest edicts from the government? "The official announcement won't be made until next week. However, *Huli* Transport is merging with Yamamoto Logistics. The main company headquarters are already in the process of being moved. To Japan."

Xi Niu gasped.

Fu Rui could tell his hold on Ao Dan wavered long enough that the older chaos wizard was able to break free. With a wave of Ao Dan's hand, Xi Niu flew across the room and landed crumpled against the foot of the sofa. The slight snore he gave almost immediately let Fu Rui know that the boy was unharmed.

However, the chaos wizard didn't flee. Possibly he'd finally understood that Fu Rui didn't meant to kill him at this point.

"So you finally woke up to the threat of the Chinese government?" Ao Dan asked, bemused.

Fu Rui shrugged. "It was always a threat. Governments will always be a threat. This time, though, there was no getting around the danger. It was time for the company to leave."

Ao Dan nodded. "I'm surprised," he said. "But it is an elegant solution. Eliminates your stiffest competitor as well as sliding you out of harm's way for the moment. Plus, yet more coffers to tap into while you finalize the program."

"We would have gone public," Fu Rui said after a

moment while the two men stared at each other. "You know that we would have to eventually. And even if it took us a while, you still would have seen it."

Ao Dan gave him a wry smile and shook his head. "No, I wouldn't have. You would have had me killed long before then. Or you would have tried to."

Fu Rui couldn't deny that possibility. The company did occasionally deal with problems using the assassin's sword and not the lawyer's pen.

After sighing deeply, Ao Dan continued. "You probably won't believe me when I tell you the truth. But I had to make sure that the announcement went out before you started sending assassins after me again. Before you had a chance to kill me."

Fu Rui stayed silent, willing the man to continue.

A crystal pendant flew off the mantel to the left, one of the unviolated places in the room.

Fu Rui had long since trained his mind to accept that it was magic he was seeing, though his conscious brain wouldn't believe it, no matter how many times he saw it. After their meeting, he'd probably "remember" Ao Dan merely handing the crystal to him.

The crystal was about the width of Fu Rui's pinky, about four inches long, with eight smooth sides. A silver loop grew out of the top of it, obviously meant to be worn. When Fu Rui held it up to the light, he saw tiny flecks of gray and black floating through the center of the piece.

"Ashes," Ao Dan explained. "Henry's ashes."

Fu Rui blinked, surprised. He hadn't expected such sentiment from Ao Dan. He'd rarely talked about his former husband—hadn't even taken any time off when he'd died. Fu Rui looked at the crystal again, then back to Ao Dan. He shook his head. He didn't get it.

"Henry's participation in the program can't be denied,

now," Ao Dan said softly. "His sacrifice will be acknowledged and remembered forever."

Fu Rui opened his mouth, then closed it again. The crystal pendant flew out of his fingers. Again, his brain refused to acknowledge that Ao Dan still stood many feet away from him, and that he'd just seen magic.

"So you got the media involved just so that Henry wouldn't be forgotten?" Fu Rui said, disbelieving.

"You would have written him out of the story," Ao Dan said. "Admit it. He isn't in any of your press releases or official histories about the project. Just as you've written me out, too."

"If you had let me know that it was that important to you, I would have made sure he was mentioned," Fu Rui said. "Especially given the threat of exposure."

Ao Dan studied him for a moment, then gave a rueful chuckle. "You may have tried. Even with the best of intentions, though, you would have failed."

Fu Rui shrugged. He wasn't perfect, he knew that. He still would have done his best. "Why are you so certain I'd fail?"

"What is the only thing that a Chinese wizard, or a Japanese wizard, or even an American wizard, hate more than each other?" Ao Dan said. When Fu Rui didn't reply, he answered himself. "A warlock of any kind."

Fu Rui didn't get it. But then again, he was completely mundane. He'd heard the arguments back and forth. He'd been the one to finally approve Ao Dan's truce, feeling at times as though he was the only adult in the room.

But that was yet another reason why mundanes sat on the board of directors. To see beyond the rivalries of wizards and keep their eyes on the profit.

"So, now that you have wrecked my home, and gotten

the answers you needed, I'm assuming that our truce is off?" Ao Dan asked.

"The Japanese have even less tolerance for a chaos wizard than the Chinese," Fu Rui admitted. "Their wildness must always be controlled."

Ao Dan merely nodded.

"Personally, I would have had you stay on the program," Fu Rui said. "But consider this your warning that your truce with *Huli* Transport is officially at an end."

"It lasted longer than I'd expected it to, quite frankly," Ao Dan said. He gave the other man a true smile. "But at least we're going to the stars."

"*Huli* Intergalactic," Fu Rui said.

"I can't wait to use your services," Ao Dan joked.

"Of course," Fu Rui said. He didn't hesitate, but gave Ao Dan a deep, formal bow, knowing that he'd never see the man again. They all owed this chaos wizard a deep debt, though he suspected that he would be the only one to ever acknowledge it.

When he straightened back up, Ao Dan was gone.

EPILOGUE

AO DAN SAT in the pilot seat of his little spaceship, facing the huge portal in front of him. Two others sat on the bridge with him, a holder and a seeker. They were both involved with their own magic, of course. The holder had an image of a swirling portal dancing above his control board, while the seeker had a similar, though rounder version on hers.

It had taken Ao Dan years to find and train other chaos wizards not just who could do the seeking and holding, but also whose company he would be able to tolerate for long enough periods of time.

While Ao Dan was capable of performing all three tasks, he felt most comfortable as pilot, in control of the ship when they went plunging through the abyss. Despite the improved shielding—more weird physics courtesy of Henry— sometimes the darkness became too much for a pilot to bear and they'd purposefully drive their ship into it.

Most of the early pilots in the program had suffered that fate, like Justin, who after years of retirement, had decided to re-enter the program for just "one more flight."

Kan Li had also died, though not because of the

program, but because she'd finally taken it upon herself to come after Ao Dan. He'd almost mourned killing her. She'd been essential to the initial success, but she was a company wizard first and foremost.

The only one of the original team still alive was Xi Niu. He'd surprised everyone by deciding to follow a management track in the company, and not stay a wizard, despite his tremendous magical strength. He'd ended up the manager in charge of the *Huli* Intergalactic American branch, overseeing the program until he'd retired, just a few years before, at the age of one hundred and thirty.

He'd even stayed in touch with Ao Dan, holding onto him as fiercely as he had the rest of those he considered family. It always surprised the chaos wizard to find Xi Niu seated across from him at a restaurant or café, half a world away from the business headquarters in Japan.

Ao Dan was never certain why Xi Niu never felt inclined to tell the rest of the corporation about how to find the chaos wizard. However, Xi Niu always assured Ao Dan that he wouldn't, and he'd kept his word.

Xi Niu was why Ao Dan now had a top-of-the-line spaceship, built out of the latest materials, with the most advanced engines and cooling systems. It still astonished Ao Dan that Xi Niu had agreed to his request.

Seemed that Xi Niu also felt that, despite their essential differences, the company owed Ao Dan a debt.

Ao Dan had also paid his own debt. Henry's name would forever be associated with the creation of the beacons. Sure, Ao Dan himself had been written out of history. He didn't care about that. He'd owed Henry, though, particularly after driving the man insane.

After killing him.

It was time, though. Time to leave Earth. Time to drift among the stars for a while. Time to set up the space station in orbit around Jupiter. Time to learn asteroid mining, at least until more beacons were placed.

Huli Intergalactic had taken the name seriously and sent out drone ships, traveling as fast as they could through normal space, dropping beacons as they went. It would take man centuries before they colonized those stars.

Ao Dan had time. He still planned on living forever, until he met his Richard again, reincarnated as his true love.

With a gleeful grin, Ao Dan pushed the tiny spaceship forward, into the future.

ABOUT LEAH R CUTTER

Leah Cutter writes page-turning fiction in exotic locations, such as a magical New Orleans, the ancient Orient, Hungary, the Oregon coast, rural Kentucky, Seattle, Minneapolis, and many others.

She writes literary, fantasy, mystery, science fiction, and horror fiction. Her short fiction has been published in magazines like *Alfred Hitchcock's Mystery Magazine* and *Talebones*, anthologies like Fiction River, and on the web. Her long fiction has been published both by New York publishers as well as small presses.

Find Leah's books on Knotted Road Press at (www.KnottedRoadPress.com)

Follow her blog at www.LeahCutter.com.

Reviews

It's true. Reviews help me sell more books. If you've enjoyed this story, please consider leaving a review of it on your favorite site.

Come someplace new…

Are you a traveler? Do you enjoy exploring strange new worlds, new cultures, new people?

Journey into the various lands envisioned by Leah Cutter.

Sign up for my newsletter and I'll start you on your travels
with a free copy of my book, *The Island Sampler*.

I will never spam you or use your email for nefarious
purposes. You can also unsubscribe at any time.

http://www.LeahCutter.com/newsletter/

ABOUT KNOTTED ROAD PRESS

Knotted Road Press fiction specializes in dynamic writing set in mysterious, exotic locations.

Knotted Road Press non-fiction publishes autobiographies, business books, cookbooks, and how-to books with unique voices.

Knotted Road Press creates DRM-free ebooks as well as high-quality print books for readers around the world.

With authors in a variety of genres including literary, poetry, mystery, fantasy, and science fiction, Knotted Road Press has something for everyone.

Knotted Road Press
www.KnottedRoadPress.com